# Across the Bleeding Sky

DON JESSEN

**Across the Bleeding Sky**

*By Don Jessen*

ISBN 979-8-838-46722-5

Front cover design by Marilyn Jessen.

# *Prologue*

September 15th, 1976

THE FLIGHT WAS going well. It was my final solo. I had flown from Hamilton to Ardmore, then onto Tauranga. The flight back over the Kaimai ranges had been a bit bumpy, but flying over the Waikato basin had been plain sailing.

Looking over the farmland north of Cambridge, I could pick up the lifestyle block that my fiancée lived on with her mother and younger brother.

Knowing she had no lectures on at University that afternoon, I altered course slightly and flew over the farmlet. Sure enough, I could see her blue Volkswagen Beetle parked in the drive. With a bit of a grin, I put the Cherokee into a slow descent.

At 1,000 ft, directly over the house, I commenced a steep turn, holding it for three circuits until I saw my beloved running from the house to watch. I saw her wave, then waggling the wings, climbed back to 2,000 feet heading for the airport and home. I was due out at the farmlet for dinner, so I justified my slight detour by thinking it had been a good way of saying, 'Hi Sweetie, I'm almost home.'

I sat comfortably in the pilot's seat of the Cherokee 140. With a nervous habit I have, I adjusted my fine, gold-rimmed glasses and ran my hand through my dark hair, which was worn fashionably long. I reached out a slim wrist, no thicker than that of a finely boned woman, and picked up the radio mic.

'Tower, this is Delta Quebec Zulu, turning final,' I said in my laconic New Zealand drawl.

'Delta Quebec Zulu, this is the tower; you are cleared for final approach and to land on runway 36. There is a 10 to 15-knot variable crosswind due west.'

'Roger that,' I acknowledged.

As a student pilot, I went into my final approach routine, pulling on 10 degrees of flap, easing off the throttle and re-trimming the aircraft. I pulled back further on the throttle and pulled on 15 degrees of flap.

I could feel the crosswind now. I crossed the boundary of the long-sealed tarmac at 250 feet, pulled on the full flaps and eased the throttle off while simultaneously easing the nose of the Cherokee slightly into the prevailing wind and slightly canting the plane's windward wing down.

I re-trimmed and as the plane sank toward the tarmac I kicked the nose and wing straight at the very last moment.

The plane's wheels gently kissed the tarmac, the nose dropped and the front wheel touched. The plane rumbled down the runway, slowing as the brakes were applied.

'Delta Quebec Zulu, this is the tower; you are cleared to leave runway 36.'

'Tower, this is Delta Quebec Zulu. Thanks for that. Delta Quebec Zulu is shutting down,' I replied.

I turned off the runway and trundled across the grass to the aircraft's designated parking area. I brought the plane to a halt and switched off.

Glancing at my watch, I found to my surprise, it was 5.05pm. I had been up longer than I thought. Must have been the headwind.

As I climbed out of the plane and started to put the tie-downs in place, another man wandered out of the club-rooms to assist.

'Hi John, how are you?' I called.

John glanced at me and said, 'Hi there. More to the point, how are you? How was the flight?'

I turned and smiled at the older man.

'Well, John, it was a bit hairy over the ranges, but from there, to here was pretty good. Hamilton to Ardmore was sweet, as was Ardmore to Tauranga. Coming over the Kaimai ranges, I was getting caught in quite a few updrafts and downdrafts, so I climbed up to 5,000 feet then dropped back to 3,000 feet once I was over the Waikato basin.'

John had been my flight instructor right throughout my training.

'Well', he said, 'that's your final cross–country out of the way. I bet that feels good.'

I nodded affirmatively as he walked back to the club-rooms with me.

'When are you coming out again?' enquired John.

I shook my head and, with a serious voice, replied, 'I

don't rightly know, John. Work is full-on at the plant, and we are expanding at a phenomenal rate, and it's only 12 weeks to my wedding, so I don't know that I will have much time to fly. I was lucky to get the afternoon off to do my cross–country. We are working Saturdays as well to try and meet demand.'

John grinned. 'Well, you just take it easy, and we will see you next time.'

As I headed for my car, I thought about my fiancée. She was a petite five–foot 1–inch, blue-eyed sun-bleached blonde and a gorgeous looking girl. She was very intelligent and quick of mind, and I felt blessed to have won her love and couldn't quite believe she had agreed to marry me. I was so looking forward to catching up with her as I did every day.

As John watched me drive away, neither of us realised that I would never pilot a plane again.

CHAPTER 1

*Another time, another place*

THE NIGHT CLASS had stopped for a five-minute break to stretch their legs. Joel sauntered up to me.

'What did you think of that session?'

I smiled. 'I thought it was pretty good. In fact, much to my surprise, I've really enjoyed the whole course.'

Joel laughed. 'Why am I surprised about that? Your lowest mark in the three exams so far is 94%. That's outstanding.'

I shrugged. 'I just guess I find the whole clinical hypnotherapy thing fascinating.'

'There's just four more classes. A final exam, then we will all be professionally qualified clinical hypnotherapists. Do you think you will practise?' asked Joel.

'I don't know,' I replied, 'I have a real problem with the next few week's sessions on past life regressions. I just don't believe in any of that stuff, and quite frankly, I don't want anything to do with it. But if I miss the lectures, I will fail the course.'

Joel looked at me. 'You are not alone in your thoughts; there are a few of us feeling the same way as you.'

Dennis, the lecturer, clapped his hands.

'Can you please take your seats again?'

He waited while we all settled ourselves, then said, 'Over the next weeks, we will be doing sessions on past life regressions. This is the final part of your diploma course.

'Now, I know a few of you are a bit anxious about it; for some of you, it will be against your beliefs, and others will just think it is plain freaky.

'However, I must tell you that whatever you think or believe, it is a relevant type of therapy, and there are many instances recorded of effecting cures on long–term phobias.

'It is a complex subject in its own right, and as a therapist, you need to know about it. There have been many recorded instances of clients spontaneously regressing into what appear to be past lives, so you also need to understand it and to be able to cope with it.

'So, for the rest of the night, I am going to conduct a group past life regression session. There is nothing like experiencing it yourselves to understand that it is non–threatening.'

A nervous murmur went around my classmates.

'Crap,' I thought to myself. 'What do I do now? Hell, man, you are forty–five years old. How about swallowing your fear because that is the real reason you don't want anything to do with this. Get a grip!'

I took a deep breath to calm myself.

I looked at Joel, sitting next to me.

He seemed nervous and quite pale. I gave him a sickly smile.

This was giving me the same feeling I had when I first flew solo all those years ago.

Dennis started his patter, and as a group, all of us students slipped into hypnosis. This wasn't difficult as we all trusted Dennis and had all been in hypnosis many times.

Dennis's quiet but firm voice carried us along.

'I want you all now to go back to a time when you were five years old. I want you to recall a happy time.'

He paused a moment.

'Now, I want you to go back to a time before you were born, a time before you were in your mother's womb. I want you to imagine you are standing in a beautiful garden and a path is leading toward an old house.

'Imagine you are travelling down that path toward the old house. As you travel, your spirit takes you back, back in time toward a previous life. You arrive at the house and enter through the door.

'A long white painted hallway stretches away in front of you. To the right are five doorways; to the left another seven. Behind each of those doorways stands a previous life. I want you to move down the hallway, and when you find a door that really attracts you, I want you to open it and step through.

'You will see a life in front of you. In this case, it will appear as a movie to you. You will see a scene, and I want you to take note of the scene, the surroundings, the clothes, and what is happening. You will see yourself and feel what you are experiencing. You will also feel completely safe, knowing that I am here to guide you.

7

'Now, walk to your doors, and I will give you some time before I call you back.'

Unbeknown to all of us, Dennis waited five minutes, maybe ten minutes, while he actively watched for any change of facial expression or any signs of distress. Then he called us back.

'I want you to now step back into the corridor. Please do as you are told. Now, shut the door you went through. As you shut the door, you will leave the life you have seen, and though retaining vivid memories of it, you will now be entering your current life.

'As you walk back down the hall to the front door and down the path to the garden, you will, with each step, be returning more and more strongly to your current life.

'As you progress through your birth, through your childhood, you become more and more grounded in your current life, whilst retaining very vividly the emotions and pictures you have just experienced in your previous life.

'As you progress through your teenage years and reach your current age, you find yourself feeling comfortable with the images and emotions of your past life experience and feel peaceful and calm as you come out of hypnosis.

'On the count of three, I will ask you to open your eyes. One. Feeling peaceful, calm and relaxed, ready to share your experience with the group. Two. Feeling good. Feeling powerful and in control. Three. Feeling happy and really alive, opening your eyes, now!'

The class stirred as we all opened our eyes.

Dennis was watching all our faces.

Everyone was relaxed, and most, along with me, were deeply thoughtful.

After many years of teaching the subject, Dennis, I think, realised that his class of '95 was no different from previous classes.

Some students would not have seen much of anything. Others would have had reasonably vivid experiences, while others would have had almost earth-shattering, life-changing experiences that would appear to have been very real in every aspect.

He smiled.

'Well, how about we go around the room and let's share what each of you experienced.'

He started on the other side of the group from me.

I was astounded at what had happened to me. The images I had seen, no, had experienced, was a better word, had been so strong I had felt I was actually living those moments. It had totally taken me by surprise. I listened with half an ear to the others explaining their experiences while trying to come to terms with what had happened to me.

'Well', asked Dennis, looking directly at me. 'What happened with you?'

I answered his question.

'I think my experience was very vivid. As soon as we entered the hallway, as you were still instructing us, the first doorway on my right burst open, and I could see biplanes, both British and German, dogfighting all over the sky. It was obviously a scene from World War 1. I could see the planes in great detail. It was as if I was really there.'

'Did you see yourself at all and notice what you were wearing,' asked Dennis.

'I remember at one point standing in a grass paddock,' I said. 'My shoulder was hurting.'

'What were you wearing?' prompted Dennis.

'A leather coat, high military boots, and a leather flying helmet. My God, I'm in a pilot's outfit,' I exclaimed.

'Did you know which side you were on?' asked Dennis.

'No idea,' I replied. 'I assume it would be British.'

'Never presume anything with a past life regression,' rejoined Dennis.

'Now, next week I would like to run the course on Friday rather than our normal Thursday, as I have a function I would like to attend. Can everyone cope with a changed date?'

He looked around the class as everyone nodded their assent.

'Thank you, that is great. Now next week, I would like a volunteer to relive the past life they have experienced in much fuller circumstances. I will guide this experience while the rest of the class takes notes. Who wants to be the guinea pig?'

Before I knew it, I had stuck up my hand.

After my initial shock at doing something so impulsive, which was most unlike me, I realised that the experience would be good for me.

Hopefully, it would overcome my fear of the subject, just like training as a pilot in my twenties had helped me overcome my fear of flying, and if I was true to myself, I was just a bit more than curious as to what might transpire.

What sort of experience or story was going to emerge?

* * *

## September 15th, 1995

NEXT WEEK, the class formed up and the students were chatting amongst themselves, many talking to me, saying how brave I was, and asking if I was nervous. There was a quiet air of barely contained excitement in the room.

This was going to be a very different session. No one knew where it would lead. Most of my fellow students expressed relief at being observers, rather than the participant.

Dennis called the class to order. Then looking directly at me asked, 'Are you ready?'

Now it was upon me, I was strangely calm regarding the regression. I nodded and took my place in the chair at the front of the class.

Dennis did an instant induction, and I slipped easily into the hypnotic state.

As he took me down the familiar path to the old white house, I found my mind racing toward the past life experience. I became annoyed with the slowness in Dennis' voice. I was having to wait for him.

As I entered the hall, the door was already open, and I could see biplanes everywhere.

Dennis' voice penetrated my subconscious mind.

'Now I want you to go to exactly the place you were last week. Standing on the field with a sore shoulder, in a pilot's uniform. I want you to tell me when you are there.'

I indicated impatiently that I was in the spot.

'Now,' continued Dennis, 'the pain you are feeling in your shoulder is going to subside and become pain-free. I want you to describe what you are wearing.'

I glanced down at my clothes. My sweatshirt and jeans were gone. I looked at my clothes in some amazement.

'I have a leather coat that comes to my knees and polished boots that almost come up to my knees. Something is funny, though. It's like I am looking through a window, through glass, as if my eyes are pushed right up against the glass.'

Dennis thought quickly. 'I want you to raise your hand to your face. Do you feel anything?'

I followed Dennis' instruction, my face instantly relaxing. Feeling very foolish, I said, 'Ah! Silly me, they are my goggles,' as my hand automatically moved as if pushing goggles up to my forehead.

For some reason I couldn't fathom, I seemed to be two people. I knew I was sitting in a chair under hypnosis, yet equally, I felt I was the person I was describing. I could feel the emotions, and I could smell hot oil and aviation fuel.

'Now, I want you to look in front of you and tell me what you see.'

I looked around me.

'I am standing on a grass paddock. I can see biplanes parked by sheds over the far side. There are men running towards me. They are wearing grey uniforms. That seems a funny colour. They are yelling at me; it seems to be a language other than English.'

Dennis' voice came through again. 'I want you to turn around and again tell me what you see.'

In my mind, I turned around and gasped out loud. 'Oh, Mein Gott!'

Dennis interrupted, 'Stay with English so that we understand. What has got your attention?'

I replied, somewhat in shock. 'There is a crashed plane, just five yards away. There is a dead pilot hanging half out of the cockpit!'

'What else can you tell me about the aircraft?'

'It's a biplane. It has two cockpits. Oh my God, it has a cross on the side of it! I think it's a German plane. Oh hell, the soldiers have reached me. They are talking to me in German, and I can understand it! They are calling me Leutnant and asking me if I am OK. I — I think I must be a pilot. A German pilot!'

Totally unaware myself, Dennis had noticed students' hands shooting up, obviously with questions or observations. He said to me, 'Now I want you to stay calm and relaxed and just be in the moment. Can you come up with your name? Can you ascertain your age? While you are doing that, I am going to talk to the class. You will be able to hear us but will remain calm and unconcerned. Until I call you again, just stay where you are.'

Dennis turned his attention to the class. I heard him ask, 'Yes, Joel, what is it?' Joel burst out, 'His face seems to have changed around the jawline and mouth.' Others joined in, commenting that they had noticed the same thing.

Another student, Luke, commented, 'His voice has changed too. He has a different accent.'

Dennis answered, 'Both your comments are valid. It's rare but not unknown for slightly physical and vocal changes to occur. It means the life our subject is experiencing was a highly significant life to him. It also means he is highly involved and emotionally connected at a very deep level to where he is at the moment. I have only seen these changes occur once before in my professional life. I think we might be in for a significant experience as observers ourselves.'

He held up his hand for quiet and spoke to me. 'This is Dennis. Can you hear me?'

I nodded.

'Can you answer the questions I asked you before?'

I again nodded. 'The officers are calling me Kurt, and I think I must be about 20 years old. I understand from the soldiers' talk that I am training to be a pilot, and this was my first trial flight. We crash-landed.'

'OK, that is great. Now, I want you to go further back in time, to a significant time that is important to you. Can you tell me where you are now?' My mind shifted to another time as a scene was revealed to me.

'I am at my uncle and aunt's house. I live with them. We are having a party. It is my seventeenth birthday. My aunt and uncle and my two cousins are here. Also, the vicar and his daughter Maria are here. I like Maria. We have been good mates forever. She is fifteen. I think my parents must have died when I was very young because I have always lived with my aunt and uncle.

'There is great excitement because I have just been accepted as a cadet to train as an army officer. I leave tomorrow.'

'Is that all that was significant at that time?' asked Dennis.

'No, no!' I exclaimed, 'There is a lot of noise outside. We are all rushing out of the house. Maria is pointing up in the sky and crying out in great excitement. We all are looking up. It is a flying machine! It is the first one I have seen. Oh, it is magnificent! I would so like to be up there in it.'

Dennis' voice cut back in, 'I would like to move you forward in time now, to the next significant time in your life. Can you tell me where you are and what has happened to you? Can you give me a time period?'

I replied. 'I am a qualified pilot and have been flying for a year. I'm a good pilot but not a very good fighter as I have yet to shoot down a plane. I mainly get to do reconnaissance work with an observer onboard. It is October 1916, and I have just been posted to a new fighter squadron. I am standing on a station to catch a train to my new squadron.'

Unaware that my voice was still narrating, I slipped completely into the life of young Kurt, a German pilot in World War One.

The class, Dennis and my current life faded away as my past life experience took over. In my mind, I was completely living and experiencing the life lived eighty years before.

# CHAPTER 2

## Maria

OCTOBER 16TH, 1916

I HEARD the whistle of the approaching train. I picked up my suitcase and moved toward the edge of the crowded platform. I was quite excited about my transfer. I was leaving behind the two-seaters I had been flying for the last year and moving to one of the newly formed single-seater Jastas.

I would be flying fighter planes, supposedly the best aircraft in the air. Jasta 11, flying under the command of Oberleutnant Rudolf Lang, was to be my new home. I wondered what it would be like.

I watched as the train pulled into the station, steaming and hissing like they always did. It bought back memories of being in the army railway regiment. I let the passengers disembark, and then, along with many other people, I climbed on board the train.

It was very crowded, and I pushed my way through the carriages looking for a seat.

The first free one I saw would sit me next to a young woman. She had her head down, reading a book, but I could see her blonde hair tumbling around her shoulders. I felt a blush rising up my face. I cursed myself for my extreme shyness around women, but taking my courage in my hands, I hesitantly said, 'Excuse me, Fraulein, is this seat taken?'

The young woman looked up at me. She was stunning. I had never seen such a beautiful face. Her blue eyes widened as she looked up at me. I was of a reed–slim physique, and even in my officer's uniform felt uncomfortable with my appearance, particularly around women. I felt my face go really crimson.

As I looked at her, I felt that we had met before. She seemed familiar. Suddenly the young woman lurched to her feet. I felt her lithe young body against mine as she flung her arms around me in a tight embrace.

'Kurt!' she exclaimed, 'Is it really you! I have so missed you.'

I pushed the young woman to arm's length and stared at her. Her voice brought back strong memories.

I said hesitantly, 'Maria, is it you?'

'Of course, it's me, stupid. Oh, it is so good to see you again. It has been nearly four years.'

She grabbed my hand and pulled me down to the seat.

With my face still crimson, I stammered, 'Maria, you have grown up. Last time I saw you, you were a flat-chested fifteen–year–old kid in pigtails. Now you have turned into the most beautiful young woman I have ever seen.'

Maria's eyes sparkled, and she smiled. I was enchanted. 'Well, I may have grown up', said Maria, 'but I am still the same old Maria underneath. Oh, Kurt, it really is so good to see you. I was so upset to find you had come home for leave when Papa and I were away visiting relatives.'

I could feel my crimson blush fading. I smiled, 'And how is the vicar?'

'Papa is fine,' replied Maria, 'but enough of that; tell me what has happened to you over the last four years.'

As I talked about the last four years of my life, interrupted numerous times by Maria, I found myself relaxing and enjoying her company more and more. We both seemed to pick up where we had left off as children. I told her about the cadet training to become an officer. I had graduated and received a commission to Leutnant in mid–April 1915.

'I was given a week's leave, and that is when I came home. It was great to catch up with Helga and Frieda and my aunt and uncle, but I really did miss not catching up with you and the vicar,' I said.

She sighed, 'I know, poor old Papa got an earful from me when we got home, but tell me what happened then? How did you get from army officer to pilot?'

'Well, I was posted to a railway regiment, and that didn't really enthral me. Do you remember on my 17th birthday we saw a flying machine fly overhead?'

Maria nodded.

'Well, since then, every time I looked skyward and saw an aircraft flying overhead, I was enthralled, and it started to become an obsession to fly,' I replied.

'So?' she asked.

'I saw an advertisement asking for volunteers to join the air service, so I asked my C.O. about it. He gave me the go-ahead, and by July, I found myself reporting to flying school.'

'What was it like, learning to fly?' prompted Maria,

'Well, my first flight was almost my last.' I chuckled. 'The instructor took me up in a two-seater for an orientation flight, which I really enjoyed. However, when we came in to land, there was a crosswind, a wind that was hitting the aircraft side on. As we touched down, a big gust hit us and the aircraft being so light, turned turtle, so I guess we kind of crashed.'

With her eyes wide, Maria asked, 'What happened then?'

'I dislocated my shoulder, but the pilot was killed outright.'

I shrugged.

'I found out that he had only graduated as a pilot himself and only had ten hours' flying time.'

'That didn't put you off,' she asked.

'No.' I replied. 'I had loved being up in the air for that flight, and I wanted more. I ended up graduating top of my intake and was then transferred to a two-seater reconnaissance group. From there, I was posted to two different groups doing the same job. Now I am on a fourth posting, this time to a single-seater fighter group.'

I stole a look at Maria. I could not believe the transformation from child to young woman over the past four years. She was still petite but had a great figure and was just so pretty. And her vibrant, bubbly personality that I had always loved was just the same. I loved the way her lips curled when she smiled.

'Kurt, are you eyeing me up?' she laughed.

I blushed, then grinned. 'I guess I am. I just can't get over the transformation. You are just so beautiful.'

Maria chuckled, 'Well, you aren't too bad yourself. You look very handsome in your uniform, and everyone is looking at your pilot's badge. Pilots are heroes in civilians' eyes.'

I blushed again. 'Pilots may be heroes in civilian eyes, but the real heroes are the pilots who have won the Pour le Mérite. They have shot down at least sixteen enemy aircraft. I haven't shot down anything, Maria. I might be a good pilot, but I appear to be a useless hunter and a poor shot. And as to being handsome, I think you are looking through rose-tinted glasses. I am not that good looking, and I am super skinny. Add being shy to that, particularly around women, and ...'

'Kurt!' interrupted Maria, 'That is enough of that. Stop putting yourself down! I think you are handsome. I always have, and I always will!'

She leaned forward, kissing me on the cheek. 'Besides, you will shoot down lots of enemy aircraft and be my hero. I have complete confidence in you. So there!'

She stuck her tongue out at me, as she had often done when we were children growing up together.

I laughed. 'Maria, you really haven't changed a bit. You still make me laugh and fill me with confidence and joy.'

She smiled and snuggled into me, still holding my hands that she had impulsively grabbed when she pulled me down into the seat. It felt so right and comfortable it was if I had known her for a thousand years.

'Maria, I've been talking all about me and have been so enamoured with meeting up with you that I have not even asked you what you are doing on this train. Where are you going?' I asked.

'Oh, Kurt, I have volunteered as a nurse aid and have been posted to a field hospital. I report later today.'

'So do I,' I replied. 'My Jasta can't be that far from your hospital. Maria, promise me to stay in touch. Will you write to me?'

Maria tightened her grip and laid her other small hand on my slim one.

'Of course, Kurt, I would like that very much. Maybe, if our leaves coincide, we could meet up as well.'

We talked some more, about how she had gone to work for a local doctor after finishing her education. He had taught her quite a bit, and when the call had gone out for nurses and nurse aides to help in frontline hospitals, then Maria, being Maria, had volunteered.

We talked about I don't know what. Conversation just seemed to flow from both of us, and when we were both quiet, I found the silence very companionable. By and by, Maria snuggled in and went to sleep with her head resting on my shoulder. It was rather pleasant.

As the train pulled into a station, a conductor walked through the carriage announcing the stop.

Maria suddenly woke up looking a bit disconcerted. 'Kurt,' she whispered, 'This is my stop. I have to get off. I'm scared; what if I can't cope?'

I stood up, pulling her along with me. I wrapped my arms around her, giving her a warm hug.

'Maria, when have you ever not coped? You will be fine.'

I looked tenderly down at her uncertain face seeing the

21

slight fear in her lovely blue eyes. I bent as she rose to her tiptoes. Without either of us realising, our lips met in the most tender of kisses, giving us both the confidence to face our respective uncertain futures, and recalling our child-hood love and lifelong friendship. We broke apart, looking deeply into each other's eyes. Maria's arms crept around my neck, she rose on tiptoes, and her lips met mine again, this time in a passionate, loving kiss. My world lurched.

The conductor's voice broke into our thoughts, breaking us apart again. Maria smiled impishly up at me, with eyes twinkling said: 'Not handsome, indeed!'

I picked up Maria's suitcase and helped her off the train. My heart and mind were both in turmoil. Maria's kiss was my first grown-up kiss, and I couldn't believe the sweetness of it. I gave her a quick hug on the platform and said, 'Write to me every month.'

'I'll write every week,' she replied, giving me a last heart–warming smile.

I climbed back on the train and regained my seat. I couldn't stop grinning. What an amazing coincidence, meeting Maria on the train. What an amazing turn of events. She had not lost any of her childhood attraction that I had enjoyed, but that kiss! I was seeing her for the first time as a woman, and as such, I realised I was deeply attracted to her in a very grown-up way.

# CHAPTER 3

# Jasta 11 — The Early Days

A MONTH passed quickly. I had been one of the first pilots to arrive at the new Jasta. I had got on well with Rupert, our new commander. His personality was similar to my own in that he was quite quiet and reserved.

My plane was a Halberstadt biplane. It was a lovely aircraft to fly, and I was soon flying it to its extremes. I really enjoyed the experience of flying. It made me feel alive, and I enjoyed honing my skill with each aircraft I flew.

Maria had written six times and had settled into the life of a nurse aid. Between the lines, I was beginning to realise that some of the wounds she was seeing were pretty horrific.

New pilots arrived, and I quickly made friends with fellow Leutnants Carl and Willi, brothers in arms. They arrived a couple of days after me. They were just 11 months apart in age and were both similar in their looks. There was no doubting that they were brothers.

Willi was the serious one of the two and, as I soon learnt, quite cautious. Carl, on the other hand, was quite laid back, but put him in an aircraft, and like me, he became one with it. Another good friend was a sergeant called Sebastion.

As fellow pilots in a small group, rank fell away, and real friendships developed amongst us young men. Sebastion was quite short in height but had quite a driving personality. He had entered the army as a private and been promoted through the ranks to Sergeant before transferring to pilot training. By mid–November, the Jasta was almost at full strength, with more pilots joining the band. I became great friends with another of the newcomers, Konstantin.

Konnie was a laid–back individual but with a very methodical brain. Everything he did was considered and carried out to the very best of his ability. It very quickly became obvious to us all that Konnie was very good on the engineering side of the planes. He had a knack with the sometimes unreliable engines and seemed to be able to turn his hand to any part of the aircraft that needed fixing or tuning. He was also a very steady pilot.

The Jasta's first big action was in November when on patrol, our flight was attacked by a vastly superior number of British planes. I realised at a glance that we were outnumbered by two to one.

My heart rate went up several notches, and I felt the familiar fear that I had experienced in the two-seaters creep into my stomach as we closed for action. I fired at a plane missing by many yards. I cursed as tracer passed over the top of my plane as a British pilot tried to shoot me down. I took evasive action, throwing the plane into a sickening dive.

With the engine screaming and the ground coming

toward me, I hauled back on the stick to level out and soon found myself out of range.

I was shaking like a leaf.

I looked around, seeing two other Halberstadts. I closed up and soon recognised Willi and Sebastion. We flew back to base in formation, touching down together still in formation. Half the flight was already back, and within fifteen minutes, the rest of the flight had landed. It had been our first large–scale action, and we were all buzzing with adrenalin but very relieved to be back on firm ground. No one had even got a bullet hole in their plane.

I received a letter from Maria saying she had a rostered day off. I subsequently checked out the hospital from the air and saw a good field close to the hospital that I could land on. I realised it was far enough behind the lines to be safe, so I approached Rudolf to see if I could borrow the two-seater training plane that the Jasta had, and have my day off to coincide with Maria's day off.

With the support of Rudolf and my fellow pilots, I took off, heading towards the hospital and Maria. I had it in my mind to take Maria flying. I had borrowed Sebastion's flying gear, as he was the smallest pilot in the flight.

As I circled the hospital grounds, I saw Maria standing at the edge of the field where I had determined to land. I eased the aircraft into a tight turn, lined up the strip and began my descent. I landed and taxied the aircraft up to the edge of the field. She watched my plane come to a stop. As I switched off and jumped down, she ran toward me. I smiled and caught her in my arms, giving her a great hug. Maria looked up at me, then kissed my lips.

'I have so wanted to do that again,' she whispered.

I bent down and gave her a long, gently loving kiss in return. 'Me too,' I murmured. We looked at each other, my eyes losing themselves in her gaze.

After a while, Maria leaned her head into my chest.

'What are we going to do with ourselves today?' she asked.

I smiled, 'Do you trust me?'

'Of course, I do. Why?'

I indicated the plane. 'How would you like to go for a flight?'

Maria looked at me in amazement. 'Really? Oh, Kurt, I would love to!

I turned toward the hospital grounds and smiled.

'We are going to have an audience,' I said, indicating some of the walking wounded soldiers and nurses lined up at the fence.

I rescued Sebastion's leather flying coat, helmet and goggles and assisted Maria into them. Walking around to the side of the aircraft that was hidden from our admirers, I grasped her small waist and lifted her onto the lower wing.

'Hop into the rear cockpit, and I will strap you in,' I called.

Maria looked at the cockpit, and I suddenly realised that it wasn't going to be so easy with a long skirt. She looked around. There was no one in sight other than me. She grabbed her skirt and pulled it up, exposing a slim leg. I gasped as I looked at a lovely slim thigh. I looked up at Maria as she placed her leg over the cockpit rim and hoisted herself in. I was experiencing feelings I had not previously experienced. I felt aroused and wanted to take Maria in my arms and love her.

'Damn,' I thought, 'Now, I'm going to have trouble focusing on flying.'

I climbed on the wing bending over to strap Maria in. Our faces were close together, and I fumbled nervously with the harness as I tightened it around her waist.

Maria laid her hand over mine and smiled at me. Every time she did that, I felt my heart lurch again. I gave her a quick kiss and then set the controls in the front cockpit. I climbed down and swung the propeller, pulled the chocks and raced around the end of the wing, climbing on the lower wing and into the cockpit as the engine spluttered into life. Letting the engine settle, I then eased the throttles forward and taxied down the field, turning into the wind.

I turned my head, giving Maria a smile. 'You ready?'

She nodded.

I opened the throttle, and the plane surged forward over the bumpy grass. I felt the tail rise, held it there while we gained speed, then lifted the plane off and climbed steadily, setting a course flying directly away from the front lines levelling off at 1500 feet.

I glanced over my shoulder at Maria as she looked over the side at the view below. I was fascinated with the way strands of her blonde hair that escaped the confines of her leather flying helmet waved in the wind drag. She turned and looked at me.

Behind the goggles, her eyes were alight with a fierce joy, and her smile was as wide as could be. I gave a huge sigh of relief. In my experience, people either loved flying or were frightened out of their wits. Maria obviously belonged to the former group.

I spied a village with a large green and dropped the

plane down, landing on the green. Villagers swarmed around the plane as I switched off. They were amazed as I helped Maria out.

'Oh, Kurt,' she gasped, 'That was absolutely amazing. I loved it.'

I grinned as I offered her my arm. We walked into the village and sat at a café and had a lovely lunch. Completely at ease in each other's company, we chatted away about anything and everything. After lunch, we wandered through the shops in the village. Maria spied a nightcap.

She said, 'Look, Kurt, what a neat nightcap. Try it on for me.'

I laughed and put the green knitted nightcap on. Maria shrieked in merriment. 'Kurt, I have got to buy that for you.'

I chuckled again, 'It can be my good luck charm. I will carry it with me when I fly.'

We returned to the plane, and after take-off, I set a course that took us further away from the front.

Soon, I spied a large field surrounded on three sides by trees. The fourth side was bounded by a stream. It was secluded but still allowed plenty of room to land. I dropped the plane down and rumbled to a stop. I assisted Maria down, and I spread our flying coats on the ground beside the stream. We sat beside the water, both suddenly shy.

Maria made the first move. She lent into me, pulling my arm around her. She laid my other hand upon her breast. I could feel the softness through the fabric of her dress. Her very nearness lifted my spirits.

'Maria,' I said, 'I think I am falling in love with you.'

'Only, think? Kurt, I know I am in love with you,' she replied.

I turned to face her. 'I have known you for as long as I can remember. Since we were children together. I have missed you over the last four years. You have become a beautiful woman, and you are the first woman I have ever kissed. I feel so comfortable in your presence, and I can't stop thinking about you. I want to be with you. When you raised your skirt to hop into the plane, I saw your leg I was overcome with lustful feelings for you.'

I blushed scarlet. 'I feel ashamed of those feelings.'

Maria reached up and gently touched my face.

'Do not be ashamed of those feelings, my dearest Kurt. I would take all my clothes off and lie with you and never feel ashamed. I love you, Kurt, with all my body, mind and soul.'

She pushed my chest so that I eased flat on my back to the ground. Maria lowered her lips to mine. I felt her lips so beautifully soft on mine and gave to her, loving her.

'Oh, Maria, I do so love you,' I murmured. 'I think in my heart I have always loved you, even when we were children.'

She smiled, 'And, I you, my sweet. I have always loved you, and I will to my dying day and through all eternity.'

We kissed again and lay in each other's arms with a deep contentment that neither of us had known before.

After some time, I glanced at my watch. 'My God, Maria, it's time we got going.'

We climbed into our flying gear, and I lifted Maria onto the lower wing. She looked down at me, then, deliberately, slowly, raised her skirt showing off her slim leg as she stepped into the cockpit.

'Next time,' she whispered, 'we will find a hotel and lie together for the whole day.' I looked up at her, hardly daring to believe what she had just said.

'Promise?'

'Promise,' she said.

# CHAPTER 4

# A New Leader

**R**UDOLF called all the pilots of our Jasta together.

'My friends, I have received a transfer to command Jasta 28. Sorry, Kurt, but I am taking the two-seater with me.'

We all laughed. 'Sir', asked Sebastion, 'Do you know who our new commanding officer will be?'

Rudolf replied, 'Yes, it is a young leutnant named von Ricthofen.'

A startled gasp came from most of us airmen present. Von Ricthofen was creating a name for himself. He flew with Jasta Bolecke, the most famous Jasta. I said, 'He has just been awarded the Pour le Mérite. It was in yesterday's papers.'

A murmur of excitement rippled through the airmen. What would this mean to each of them? What would their new leader be like?

Von Ricthofen arrived on January the 20th, 1917. A lone Albatross came straight in and landed. The pilot jumped to the ground, and as he pulled off his flying helmet, Konstantin recognised von Ricthofen from the photo in the papers. He alerted his fellow pilots, and we stumbled out of the mess and lined up. Straightening our uniforms, we came to attention.

Manfred von Ricthofen sauntered across to the men, studying us as he walked. Little did I know that he was wondering how he would train these underachievers in aerial warfare. Studying our profiles had indicated most were experienced pilots, but we were totally lacking in any success with shooting down the enemy.

It was something pilot training didn't cover. We learnt to fly, not hunt. Ricthofen, apparently, had decided we would soon learn, or he would transfer us. He did realise, however, that he was going to have to personally train each of us. Of course, at the time, we knew nothing of this.

At that moment, a large car swung into the airstrip. Manfred smiled. It was his orderly with his gear and a great big wolfhound.

The huge dog bounded up to him, and, taking it by the collar, he fronted up to his pilots for the first time.

'I am your new commanding officer, Manfred von Ricthofen.'

The Pour le Mérite hung conspicuously at his collar. We all let our eyes rest there for a minute before taking in the Knight's Cross and the 1st and 2nd class Iron Crosses.

'This is Moritz', he said, indicating the wolfhound.

Manfred spoke. 'Gentlemen, Jasta 11 has so far not distinguished itself in any shape or form. That is going to change. I intend to teach you the art of aerial warfare. How to hunt and shoot down the enemy! Some of you will succeed under my tuition; others will not. Those of you who do not match my expectations will be transferred out of the Jasta. Do I make myself clear?'

There was total silence.

'Well?' asked Manfred.

'Yes, Sir!' we all chorused.

'Good.' said Manfred.

He walked to the end of the line.

'Now, I need to put names to faces. You are?'

'Sergeant Sebastion Festner, Sir.'

He moved along the line, Moritz, his giant wolfhound following his every move. He finally came to me.

As he looked at me, Moritz pushed past Manfred and sat down in front of me and started to lick my hand. Manfred stared in disbelief. Moritz had always been stand-offish with other pilots. It was the first time the dog had actively approached a fellow pilot.

I felt myself blush as von Ricthofen stared at me, then stared at the dog, and returned to stare at me again. His eyes rested on my face.

I felt my blush deepening. I was acutely aware of the dog licking my hand.

'Name?'

'Kurt Wolff, Sir.'

'Hmmm, you look more like a delicate little flower to me. There isn't much of you, is there?'

'I might be thin, Sir, but I am a good flier.'

Manfred smiled.

'Well, you must be alright. Moritz is a great judge of character, and you are the first person he has ever walked right up to, let alone licked.'

He turned to the men, chuckling.

'The wolfhound likes the 'Wolfcub'. It must be a good omen, eh? I am going to settle in today. I would like to personally interview you all this afternoon.

'Tomorrow I will take you up in the air and follow you one at a time. I wish to study your flying technique.'

He paused, then carried on.

'The following day will be back to the classroom where I will teach you tactics and aerial warfare. After that, you will accompany me in ones or twos into battle, where I will show you by example how to fight. After that, I will expect results from you. Understood?'

'Yes, Sir!' we chorused.

'Good. You are all dismissed.'

Manfred strode off to his new quarters, calling Moritz to follow.

The massive dog looked up at me, wagged his tail and wandered off after Manfred.

'Thunder and lightning!' exclaimed my friend Carl, 'that was a lecture and a half. I think our lives are going to be very different from now on.'

'I think that is an understatement,' rejoined his brother Willi.

Konstantin said thoughtfully, 'I think this guy might be good for us all. Certainly, there will be more excitement around here.'

He turned to me with a twinkle in his eye.

'What do you think, my delicate little flower?'

The other pilots laughed, and I joined in with them.

'I think that somehow I am going to be stuck with that title.'

I laughed again. 'I also agree with Konstantin. It is going to be different. I think we can all learn a lot from him. After all, he is Germany's highest-scoring ace that is still alive. Besides, I like him.'

Konstantin and Carl linked arms with me as we walked back to the mess. Carl called over his shoulder and chuckled to the other pilots, 'Well, the delicate little flower says it going to be good, so it must be so.'

My interview with Manfred took place around 3pm. He looked over my file.

'I see you started your pilot training in 1915 and crashed on your first flight. Still kept learning. The crash didn't scare you off?'

I replied, 'No, Sir. We came in with a crosswind, and my instructor messed up the landing, killed himself and dislocated my shoulder bone. Didn't really put me off at all.'

'Why did you transfer from the railway corps to the air service?' he asked.

'On my seventeenth birthday, an aeroplane flew over our home. I determined at that moment I would fly, but I had already enlisted in the officer cadet training. In 1915, I got the opportunity to transfer to the air service.'

Von Ricthofen studied my file, then looked up at me.

'I see you were posted to reconnaissance squadrons flying two-seaters. Did you see any action?'

'Yes, Sir, we were shot at lots from the ground and were attacked twice by other aircraft where we exchanged rifle shots.'

'Did you apply to transfer to Jasta 11?'

'No Sir, my observer was badly wounded by ground fire, and when the request came in for the best pilots to form the new single-seater fighter squadrons, my name was put forward by my commander, mainly because I was the most experienced pilot in our Jasta.'

'I see you have logged 120 hours' flying time; that's pretty high. I will see you on the airfield at 9am tomorrow. Dismissed.'

I saluted and left through the door, giving Konstantin the thumbs up as he entered next.

The following morning, I was kitted up and standing by my aircraft when Manfred arrived. His wolfhound was in attendance, and it bounded up to me, sat back on its haunches and started licking my hand again.

Manfred called, 'Moritz, heel boy.'

The dog looked over its shoulder at von Ricthofen, then deliberately turned around and sat beside me.

By this time, I was highly embarrassed.

Manfred stopped in front of me. A slight smile twitched on his lips.

'Kurt, I think I am going to like you. Moritz sure as hell does, and what he likes, I usually like. Shall we go flying? I will follow you. Two circuits around the aerodrome steep turn at each end and two landings, then up to 4,000 feet and I will do a mock attack on you. You are to take evasive action and try and get into an attack position. Understand?'

I nodded. The first part would be easy, the second a bit more difficult, but getting into an attack position on one of Germany's best pilots? Now, that would be interesting!

Once airborne, I settled down with the flying being such a joy. The low–level steep turns went without a hitch, as did the landings and take-offs. A signal from Manfred sent me soaring to 4,000 feet. I looked to my side, and there was Manfred, easily keeping pace with me.

The Albatross he flew was clearly superior to my kite. It was a beautiful looking aircraft, and I felt quite envious. At 4,000 feet, Manfred commenced his attack. He was very aggressive, but I had plenty of experience avoiding attacks, and I smoothly jigged my kite all over the sky time and time again, getting away from him, but I just could not turn the tables on him.

Every time I tried, he was all over me. He signalled me to land, we touched down, and as I switched off, I saw Willi take off, with von Ricthofen following.

As I had been first up, the other pilots crowded around, 'How did it go?' they all chorused.

'Not good,' I replied. 'The first part was easy, and at 4,000 feet, he did some very aggressive mock attacks on me, which I managed to avoid, but every time I tried to attack him, he was all over me. If he was the enemy, I wouldn't have survived. He is really good.'

I watched all the other pilots fly and had a quiet satisfaction knowing that Carl and I had been the best of our group on the day.

THE PILOTS TOOK their seats in the mess. This was the day Manfred was going to talk tactics and aerial warfare. He had ordered all the pilots to come in casual gear. Most of us had our uniforms on with our flying jerseys over top.

Manfred strode in and took a position in front of a

blackboard. He turned to all of us pilots, took us all in at a glance, and then shook his head as he spotted me.

'Kurt, what the hell is that thing on top of your head?'

I blushed, 'ah, it's a nightcap, Sir. Kind of a lucky charm.'

Willi joined in. 'His girlfriend bought it for him, Sir. He wears it everywhere.'

'Even takes it up in his plane, Sir,' added Konstantin.

'He and the hat are kind of the Jasta's talisman, Sir,' added Carl, lamely.

'I see,' said Manfred, 'Well, if you lot set so much store by our little flower and his strange hat, then I guess I will just have to get used to it. Now let's get serious, gentlemen. My goal for this Jasta is to inflict the greatest possible damage to our enemy with the minimum losses to our own force. However, this will not be without risk.

'I have talked over your experience with you individually, and I have watched you fly. Some of you are fliers like myself; some, like Kurt and Carl, have a special touch. However, being a great flier will not help you shoot down aircraft.

'You have to become hunters. That means you have to think like hunters. You are all lacking experience in fighter attacks and hunting, so we will need good tactics when flying together.

'There needs to be a first attacker and a second plane that defends the tail of the attacker. You all need to be able to attack and defend. You always look out for your friends.'

His tone was brisk. He had a no-nonsense air about him and, as we had all learnt, was a driven man. His personality dominated the room, yet there seemed to be quite a humorous side to his personality as well.

'One of the things that has become glaringly obvious is that you all, without exception, have begun your attacks at 150 to 200 yards away from your enemy. You will never score that way. You need to close within 50 yards before you attack. Your guns will become lethal at that range.'

'When we take the whole flight up, we will fly in formation with me in the lead. We will work on a series of hand signals to indicate my intentions. Any questions so far?'

I raised my hand.

'Sir, when we are formation flying, and you attack, it will be very hard to recognise your plane once we are dog fighting. The ribbons currently used are very hard to see at times.'

'Good point,' said Manfred, 'I will give it some thought. Oh, I forgot to mention, next month the Halberstadt aircraft you currently fly will be replaced with new Albatross D3s.'

A ripple of excitement swept around the room. The new Albatross was the latest fighter and was reputed to be something special. We had all admired Manfred's example.

THE NEXT DAY, Manfred arrived at the mess and called out to me. 'I've overcome the recognition problem. Come and have a look. In fact, you all better come.'

We trooped after Manfred towards the hangar. Sitting in the foreground was Manfred's Albatross. It was freshly painted in bright scarlet red!

There was a collective horrified gasp from the pilots.

'Sir, what have you done?' asked Carl. 'No one could miss you in a plane that colour!'

Konstantin joined in, 'Sir, you will become such a target in that kite.'

Manfred replied, 'Well, I don't think the camouflage paint works at all, and this way, you will all recognise me easily.'

'Maybe, Sir, we could paint our planes similar colours to avoid the enemy singling you out,' I suggested.

'What about us painting our planes red, with maybe small parts painted a different colour so that we can readily identify each other in the air?' questioned Sebastion.

Manfred glanced around at his men. I could see he appreciated our concern for him and our willingness to paint our planes, thus sharing the danger with him.

He smiled. 'I will think about it overnight. Now, Carl and Kurt, I want you to come on morning patrol with me. We will take off in 30 minutes.'

Carl and I nodded our agreement. Thirty minutes later, our three aircraft took off and formed up together at 1,000 feet. With Ricthofen in the lead in his brightly painted red Albatross, I concentrated on staying in formation.

The air was bumpy, with the aircraft rocking around quite a bit. We climbed to 4,000 feet. Ten minutes into our flight, I noticed Manfred pointing down. I glanced over the side of my cockpit and spied five British aircraft about 2,000 feet below us.

Manfred led us in a dive from out of the sun toward the aircraft. I could feel the ice-cold wind rushing around me.

My heart was beating rapidly, and I was scared. Inside

my gloves and boots, my hands and feet were running with sweat. Beside me, Carl was holding pace.

As Manfred closed the enemy, he signalled us to go either side of him. Manfred closed to within 50 yards before opening fire. Sixty yards further back, both Carl and I opened fire.

Suddenly it was all on. The British planes swung around to fight. Von Ricthofen was in the thick of it, whilst Carl and I remained on the outskirts. With tracer flying everywhere, von Ricthofen broke off the engagement and, with us flying in formation, flew back to base. I was excited with the day. Manfred was a brave and intrepid fighter.

We landed in tight formation. Carl and I leapt from our planes and ran across to Manfred. We were both very excited.

' Well done, Sir,' called Carl.

As we neared the plane, we both stopped in horror. Manfred's plane was riddled with bullet holes and pieces of torn fabric fluttered from the wings. Manfred followed our gaze. He smiled grimly at us, then pointedly walked to each of our planes and inspected them. Not a bullet hole could he find in either of our aircraft.

He looked at us both. 'We will fly again this afternoon.'

By this time, both Carl and I were shuffling in embarrassment.

Without saying another word, Manfred stalked off to his quarters. I looked up at Carl. 'I don't think we impressed him.'

Carl furrowed his brow; 'I know we didn't. I feel like a naughty little schoolboy who has just been caught out.'

I said, 'Carl, his actions have had a huge impact on me. Much more so than if he had bawled us out.'

'Me too,' replied Carl. 'I think we are going to have to fly right with him up to that 50-yard mark.'

I thought about it for a minute, then walked around Manfred's plane again, taking in the bullet holes. This was a whole new way of fighting. Much riskier than before. I took a deep breath, 'Carl, we have to fight like him. I think it is a case of feeling the fear and just doing it anyway.'

'I agree,' replied Carl. 'If we don't, we will be transferred out of here, and that would not look good on our records. Kurt, let's shake on it. No backing down from now on.'

I thrust my hand into Carl's. Little did I know it, but the past moments were pivotal for both Carl and myself, with our example in the future dictating the way the Jasta responded to Manfred's leadership style.

The afternoon flight followed a similar pattern until we fell into an attack. This time both Carl and I held our nerve and closed to within 50 yards of our quarry before shooting.

It was as scary as all hell. The fight was fierce, with no scoring on either side, but bullets flying everywhere. I was aware of them striking my plane and prayed one would not hit me.

I seemed to be throwing the joystick around in all directions as I jigged the aircraft around the sky, trying to avoid being hit yet at the same time trying to get an enemy aircraft in my sights.

I was firing my machine-gun in short bursts. My bullets struck home on some planes but didn't seem to affect them.

By the time the engagement ended, I was wet with sweat. I had been really scared going in for the attack, but the excitement had boosted my adrenalin to such an extent that the fear had disappeared.

Now it was over, I started to shake like a leaf in a high wind, and the fear came back like a tidal wave.

On the flight back, Manfred glanced at us, both holding station beside him. He could see a row of bullet holes through the fuselage of Carl's plane, and on the other side, the fabric on my lower wing was in tatters, with one of the wing struts chewed up badly by bullets. He smiled grimly. He probably thought, 'What a change in these two from the morning.'

Me, I was shit scared and praying my kite would hold together and get me home.

On landing, he walked around the two planes again.

'Well, gentlemen, I think you will do. Two things, you can paint your planes red, with a different colour to highlight it, and I think today you earned the right to address me by my given name, Manfred.'

I looked at Carl, and he gave me a shaky grin. I gave him the thumbs up with an equally shaky grin. I guessed he was feeling exactly like I was.

# CHAPTER 5

# New Friends and New Success

FEBRUARY AND MARCH 1917

THAT NIGHT, Carl and I spent painting the aeroplanes. Carl did the main body in the same red paint as Manfred's.

He painted his rudder, ailerons and nose white, while I decided to go with a green accent. Having a little difficulty in obtaining paint, I finally did my colour in what could only be described as close to lime-green as it was possible to get. Unfortunately, there wasn't enough red, so I mixed it with other colours and ended up with a bright purple.

The next morning we wandered into the mess for breakfast, and spying Manfred eating with all the others, Carl called out.

'Morning, Manfred.'

I echoed his call. 'Morning, Manfred.'

The other pilots looked up in surprise. Manfred smiled, 'Morning, Carl, Kurt. Gentlemen, these two have earned the right to address me by my first name. When you have proved yourselves to me, you too will be able to address me by my given name, regardless of your rank. After breakfast, we will take the whole flight up, and then this afternoon, I will take Sebastion up for some tuition. Kurt, Carl, I presume your planes are ready to go?'

'Yes,' we chorused.

The mechanics had readied the planes placing Carl's next to Manfred's and mine on the other side. As the pilots trooped out, the three coloured planes were highly visible. Our fellow pilots stopped and looked.

'Oh, I forgot to mention,' said Manfred, 'You also get to paint your plane red with your own identifying colours added when you have proved yourselves to me.'

He turned to Carl. 'The white looks nice.'

He glanced at my plane. 'What the hell have you done to your crate?' he exclaimed, 'that's the most hideous colour match I have ever seen. Lime green and bright purple! And you thought my all red kite would standout!'

He gave me a gentle slap on the shoulder. 'Well, I certainly won't lose you now,' he grinned.

I smiled.

The flight took off with Carl and me flying wingmen for Manfred. Spotting several British planes, the flight broke into attack mode and dived down. I lined up and fired from 50 yards.

I saw my bullets puncture the other plane before it plunged out of sight. I swooped down to follow but saw the enemy plane making a beeline for the British lines. I broke off and searched the sky above and below.

Off away, I saw Carl fire a long burst into a two-seater and watched it fall from the sky. I was excited for Carl. It was his first kill and the first since Manfred had arrived. That night there was a huge celebration in the mess for Carl's first kill.

Unfavourable weather hampered flying in the latter part of the month, much to our frustration, but Manfred bought down another two aircraft, and Sebastion claimed his first two kills. He immediately painted his plane red with a bright purple nose and rudder. Manfred's lessons had certainly paid off for Sebastion, and as a mere sergeant, he revelled in being able to call his commanding officer, Manfred.

On February the 21st, a newcomer arrived at the Jasta. Another Karl, who already had a few kills and his new plane was immediately able to be painted red. Charlie, as he preferred to be called, painted his plane red with black trim. Charlie became fast friends with Carl, Willi, Konnie, Sebastion and me. His was another driving, fun personality, but he fitted into our group exceptionally well. We were fast becoming a group within the group. Although we all got on with everyone as a group, we were getting particularly close.

March entered its first days, and it was a month that would see a change in the Jasta. I was feeling a bit down as other pilots were starting to get results, yet no matter how hard I tried and no matter how many bullets I shot into enemy aircraft, nothing happened.

On the fourth morning of March, the British Royal Flying Corp were up in force, and Manfred ordered up two flights from Jasta 11. Charlie shot down a plane in the morning, with Manfred taking another down later in the morning. They seemed almost effortless in the way they dispatched the enemy. That feeling was further enhanced when the afternoon turned into a very successful day with Manfred shooting down another plane and Charlie taking out another two. These two were really good, and it made the rest of us pretty frustrated.

March the 6th dawned with clear skies, and Jasta 11 took to the air in numbers. In the late morning, Charlie shot down another two aircraft, which Eduard nicknamed the 'Bullet Catcher', taking a flesh wound and completing a forced landing. Eduard was always in the thick of dog fights, but like me, Willi and Konnie had not yet been successful in the air. It certainly wasn't from lack of effort from any of us.

Flying the same afternoon in a patrol, we saw a two-seater, a British BE2. Manfred indicated for me to attack, and dropping in behind it, I opened fire with a long raking burst. I saw the plane take my bullets and then spiral earthwards. Feeling elated, I grinned, 'At last.'

Suddenly, my aircraft bucked as a British plane opened fire from behind.

In a panic, I threw the joystick sideways and rolled the plane in a wildly descending spin, escaping unscathed. I flew low and spied the plane I had attacked, crashed in a field.

I flew back to base wildly elated. Manfred and Carl arrived in shortly after, with Manfred having claimed another victory.

With the Jasta celebrating its victories in the early evening, Manfred was raising his glass of wine when a motorcycle pulled up outside. A tall leutnant stepped off the machine.

'Oh! Here's trouble!' Manfred grinned as the lanky officer walked into the mess. 'Gentlemen, may I introduce our newest recruit, Leutnant Lothar von Ricthofen, my younger brother. Lothar, you are just in time to join our celebrations. We have shot down four aircraft today. Gentlemen, a toast to our success!'

The Jasta pilots raised their glasses and drank.

'Another toast, gentlemen. To our delicate little flower, Kurt, on his first victory. May there be many more!'

The pilots raised their glasses and, with great gusto, replied, 'To our delicate little flower!'

I coloured up with a blush. Lothar looked across at me and immediately crossed the room.

'Let me be the first to shake your hand,' he cried.

I stretched out my hand and grasped Lothar's. It was the start of a great friendship between the two of us.

Nine days into March, Manfred was leading a flight when we spotted a formation of British planes. Fifty yards out from his target, Manfred's plane was attacked by a British aircraft and shot through the fuel tank. He shut down and glided away to a forced landing. The fight continued after Manfred's departure. Charlie shot down another two FE8s, but his plane was badly shot up, and he peeled away to try and find a spot to land his damaged plane.

Carl and I continued the fight. I got in behind my target and fired a long burst. The FE8 spiralled to the ground. My second victory! I peeled away to see another

FE8 go down in flames from Carl's guns. It was Carl's second victory as well.

We flew home together, delighted in our morning's work. That afternoon, using my aircraft, Manfred brought down his 25th plane. Another five kills for Jasta 11. It was hard to come to grips with. Following Manfred's advice and direction, our little non–performing Jasta was starting to get results.

Of course, Manfred and Charlie were setting a great example, and it was hard not to be inspired by them. We were all starting to throw ourselves into close aerial combat, and it was a different skill set that we had to master. I had started to notice that Lothar was very aggressive in the air and a tad reckless with it. But that was his personality type on the ground. He was a very happy–go–lucky type of person.

The following day, Manfred, flying with Lothar on a tutoring mission, shot down his 26th enemy aircraft. We also had replacement Albatross aircraft delivered. They were a beautiful looking aircraft with plywood fuselages rather than fabric. My friends all decided that I should be the first to paint my new aircraft so that it would be bright red, in keeping with the rest of the Jasta, rather than the oddball in ugly purple. It looked really smart in bright red and lime green.

The next two days were spent with the Jasta painting the Albatross and learning to fly them. They were such a step up from the old Halberstadt. I just loved my new aerial steed and soon had it flying to its limits above the airfield. Manfred had also come up with a new idea.

Up until now, we had been taking off individually and

getting into formation once airborne. Manfred got us to line our aircraft up in formation on the ground. Once started, we held the aircraft in that formation. A ground crew waved a flag then we all opened the throttle at the same time, taking off in formation.

After several practices, we got it right and found, as Manfred had suspected, that we saved a lot of time, with our patrol time being longer and our response time being shorter. The turbulence from the aircraft being so close together made for bumpy take-offs, but nothing we couldn't handle.

Manfred really was a master tactician.

By March the 29th, Manfred's total was up to 31. On his return to base that day, he found he had been promoted to the rank of oberleutnant, some six months ahead of other officers with the same date of commission. In the middle of March, Charlie had shot down two more planes, with myself taking down my third one. My friend Lothar earned his first victory toward the end of March.

On March the 30th, Jasta 11, having taken off in formation, we as a group spied a number of French Nieuports. Stealthily, we crept up on them using cloud cover to hide our approach.

The air was bumpy, and the temperature was cold. I wiped my oiled, spattered goggles with my scarf to clear my vision. As we dived with engines screaming, the Nieuports split formation, but not before I lined one up and raked it with my machine-gun. The Nieuport rolled and spiralled away in flames.

I rolled my Albatross around to rejoin the fight, but it was all over. That afternoon my friend Carl shot down another plane, His third, but at the same time, the 'Bullet Catcher' finally caught one too many and was killed.

Eduard was Jasta 11's first casualty. That night the mess was very subdued as we toasted Eduard. It had suddenly brought the war and its deadly effect very close to home. We were all very sad.

The last day of March saw me avenge Eduard's death when I brought down an FE2b two-seater. One crewman was killed and the other taken prisoner. These are a strange pusher aircraft with a forward-mounted machine-gun and a rear-facing machine-gun mounted on the top wing. Both were operated from the front cockpit.

Take out the gunner, and the aircraft was cold turkey. I came in stealthily from the rear lower quarter unseen, then fired a burst from close quarters into the front cockpit, taking out the gunner, flicked the Albatross around and came back firing on the now defenceless aircraft concentrating on the exposed pusher engine. When it faltered, I trailed it down to watch it land behind our lines.

I BROUGHT MARCH to a close, having become an ace and having collected five souvenir pieces acquired from each of my victories. It was hard to take in. I had gone from a 'nobody' to an ace in just a few weeks. The pride I felt and the friendships I had built, along with the pure joy of flying, were beginning to override the terrible fear I felt in the dogfights.

That day, Carl, Charlie and I all learned that we had been awarded the Iron Cross 1st class.

I wrote to Maria.

'My dearest Maria, the last fortnight has been very busy for our Jasta. Lothar shot down his first plane, and Charlie has had an outstanding month. His total now stands at eight. My good friend Carl now has three victories, and my own total now stands at five. Yes, my dear, I have shot down four more enemy aircraft since I last wrote to you.

'We have just heard that Carl and Charlie have been awarded the Iron Cross 1st Class and that I am to receive both the Second Class and 1st Class Iron Crosses. Carl and Charlie already have the Second Class Iron Cross, awarded during their cavalry days. Manfred is very pleased with our efforts.

'Oh, I forgot to tell you, we have all painted our crates red to match Manfred's, but all have added flashes of colour so we can identify each other in the air. Most of us have painted the nose cone, wheels and tailplane, though Konnie has gone red with white wavy lines on the latter half of his fuselage. Lothar has used a bright yellow, Carl white, Charlie black, Willi a dark blue, and Sebastion has used purple. My colour choice of accent, which I think is very dashing, is a very vivid lime green.

'My Sweet, I am really missing not being able to see you, talk to you and hold you in my arms again. My dearest hope is that we can secure a day or two off where we can be together once more. Yours in love, Kurt.'

As I sat passively in my room, quietly surveying with a grim satisfaction my souvenirs from my five 'kills', I heard a voice from far, far away.

It seemed to be beckoning me. It was like I was a fish on a hook and was being reeled in.

The voice became more insistent, and suddenly I found myself back in a chair, split between two lives.

I heard Dennis say, 'What happened next?'

I started to reply and immediately plummeted back into the life of Kurt, a young German aviator, becoming totally immersed once again.

# CHAPTER 6

# Bloody April

APRIL 1917

A PRIL HAD started well for me. On the second and third day, I managed to down two aircraft by coming on them from the sun's rays, thus hiding myself to some extent. They were my two easiest victories to date.

Picking off a solitary aircraft was a much easier task than formation fighting, where planes were all over the sky shooting at each other. I had been on patrol with Konnie as my wingman. I signalled my intentions and dropped into a dive.

The Englishman didn't know what hit him when I fired from close range. The second flight was a repeat of the first, with Willi flying as my wingman. I mentioned to Manfred how easy it had been and wondered if the British pilots were very new to aerial warfare as neither of them appeared to notice me until I had opened fire.

On the 5th, we were ordered to strafe trenches, work I

hated. Although it helped our troops, I always felt awful, as we had an unfair advantage over the troops below us. The only excitement was a lone enemy plane that had the audacity to attack our five planes. We made it very warm for him, but he managed to evade us at a very low altitude.

Later that morning, Manfred shot down two planes and Georg and Sebastion one each.

On the 7th, the Jasta got the good news that Manfred had been promoted to the rank of captain. We celebrated with a flight where Manfred shot down another victim.

The Jasta's score was beginning to mount. Clear skies on Sunday saw us up again. The air was so still, it was as if we were just floating. This part of our sorties was pure joy to me. Being in the air, just floating along, listening to the beat of our engines.

The only thing that gave a sense of forward motion was the cold wind created by our machines. It was icy on the exposed flesh of my face. It was afternoon, and word had come of a bombing raid by four two-seater DH4 bombers. We were sent to intercept.

I was flying with Charlie, and as we spotted the bombers, we both singled one out and went in for the attack.

For the first time, the fear that had plagued me when attacking was not present. Instead, an icy calm came over me. My mind went to a single track as I stalked my quarry. I closed from above at the rear.

The machine gunner opened up at me, but his bullets were wide. Closer I came to the bomber, then at 50 yards opened up. My machine-guns raked the bomber, and down she went.

I put my crate into a dive and followed her down, watching her crash in a field below. It was my 8th victim. I felt a grim satisfaction. No elation, just a grim satisfaction of a job well done. It was a strange feeling, almost a detachment from reality.

On returning to the airfield, I found Charlie had also been successful in downing his 13th enemy plane. On the 9th, Charlie shot down another plane to claim his 14th victory.

News that a friend of Manfred's, Werner Voss, had been awarded the Pour le Mérite came through. He had dropped in a few days previously, and we had all got to meet him. At 19 years old, he was the youngest pilot to earn the Pour le Mérite. That night the alcohol was dispatched in quantity. It was good to celebrate his success, but in reality, we were all hiding our feelings behind bravado, desperately giving vent to the ongoing stresses.

The following Wednesday was a great day for our group of fliers, with the Jasta recording seven victories.

On our patrol, Sebastion and Charlie both downed one each, with Lothar and I both engaging and successfully downing one enemy aircraft each.

Fifteen minutes after landing, I had refuelled and was flying wingman to Manfred, where I had the honour of watching him take his 40th victory.

The next day, Manfred deemed it to be a day off, as the weather wasn't that great, with rain falling on the ground. I borrowed Lothar's motorbike and rode to the hospital, where I was able to take lunch with Maria.

It was just great to lay eyes on her again. We talked about the war and how Jasta 11 was featuring in the news.

She was very proud of my efforts in the air. I tried to explain to her how I felt. I was proud of my record but, at the same time, was melancholy about the pilots who had died. Even though they were enemy, we had met and entertained three of them who had survived being shot down. We had come to realise that they were not that different and, like most of us, loved flying.

It is strange to feel both elated and sad over the same event. All too soon, lunch was over with Maria going back to work and myself astride the motorbike riding back to the aerodrome.

The next day dawned, and I felt that it was going to be a special day.

A report of six RE8s within striking distance came in, and Manfred, Lothar, Sebastion and I took to the air. We soon spotted them and dived upon them. As we dived, we were joined by an Albatross from another Jasta. Each of us singled out a plane and attacked.

The RE8s were not highly manoeuvrable, so they were easy targets. Dodging bullets, we all closed and opened fire. Again the icy calm came to me as I stalked my prey. Five of the planes disintegrated before our eyes, crashing to the ground. As the sixth plane tried to bolt, Lothar went after it, bringing it down.

It took our individual totals to Manfred 41, Lothar 5, Sebastion on 9 and myself to 10. Manfred scored another two victories that day, and my good friend Charlie claimed his 17th victory, with Sebastion claiming his 10th.

It had become a competition amongst us pilots, with all of us counting our victories and collecting souvenirs of our kills. It was kind of macabre, but by taking this line of thought, it helped us keep at bay the dread of being shot down and thoughts of the British and French pilots we were killing. Also, the rewards of medals and recognition were kept out in front of us to keep our motivation up.

That night I started a letter to Maria.

'My Darling Maria, today I scored my tenth victory in the air. All the guys are congratulating me, slapping me on the back and buying me beers at the mess. Everyone is very upbeat on the surface. In the air, I have become icy calm and have developed a real sense of detachment when in action. That stays with me until after I have landed. If I can, I go and find the downed plane and collect a souvenir piece of the aircraft. Back at base, I place it with the other bits of planes I have salvaged. It's a grim hobby I've developed.

'At night, I wake up in cold sweats and find myself shaking. My roommate Charlie tosses and turns at night and cries out in his sleep. I think the killing is getting to me. I think about the British pilots who have lost their lives. It could be me, Maria.'

Flying patrol on the 13th, our group shot down another eight planes. I brought down four of them. I took out a Bristol, another RE8, a Martinside and a Nieuport. The day had been cloudy, and I had used the clouds to good effect as I stalked my prey, being able to get close in before they realised I was there. I was now extremely comfortable in my Albatross and could fly it to its extremes.

On these days, the love of flying, stalking, and then outflying my adversary overrode any fear I felt. My mind seemed to become crystal clear and ice cold. I was now pretty sure the British and French were fielding a lot of newly trained inexperienced pilots. How could they not be aware of us?

I spent every minute in my machine scanning the sky around me. Then I remembered my own early days. My commander of my first unit once went up on patrol with me and, on our return, asked how many enemy aircraft I had spotted. I replied that I had seen five and was shocked when he told me he had seen fifteen.

The next day saw us move airfields from La Brayelle to an airfield at Roucourt, southeast of Douai. The higher-ups believed British planes were causing havoc in the area, so we were moved to counteract the British build-up.

Back up in the air, the same day saw my friends and I bring down another four aircraft. Of twelve enemy shot down in two days, six had fallen to my guns! I seemed to be leading a charmed life, with my score mounting rapidly.

On the 16th, I took off with Willi and Konnie and soon spied a lone Nieuport. I put my Albatross into a steep dive and, with wing wires humming, streaked down on him like an avenging eagle. He didn't even see me until I was right on him. A long raking burst of my machine-gun soon ended him. I pulled out of the dive at low altitude and saw him crash below. I smiled with grim satisfaction as I saw the French pilot scramble from the wreck only to be surrounded by a patrol of our soldiers. I flew low overhead and rocked my wings.

Bad weather prevailed for a few days, and being land-based made all of us edgy and irritable.

I used the time to continue my letter.

'Hello, Maria, back again. We have been grounded by the weather. We are all getting snappy with each other, so

Manfred has organised some ground action. He has somehow got his hands on six motorcycles, and along with Konnie's and Lothar's motorcycles, we have eight. A track has been set up on the landing strip, and we have been ordered to go motorcycle racing. It will certainly take our minds off the war. Oh, I hear them calling me. Wish me luck in the motorcycle race.'

I tumbled outside and grabbed the motorcycle allocated to me. It was a huge amount of fun with a lot of aggression and competitiveness coming forth, along with a lot of tumbles on the corners. It was almost as exciting as flying our aircraft and was exactly what we needed.

Later that day, we welcomed a new pilot into our midst. His name was Otto, and he already had earned the Knight's Cross in his previous Jasta. His friendly disposition quickly made him a popular and accepted member of our tight-knit group. That night we had a little celebration to accord Charlie and Lothar the rights to being crowned our motorcycle racing champions.

I got up and spoke on behalf of the Jasta.

'On behalf of the Jasta 11 Motorcycle Racing Club duly formed today, it is my honour on behalf of our fellow racers to award Leutnant Charlie Schafer and Leutnant Lothar von Ricthofen the honour of motorcycle champions. As is the long-standing tradition in this newly formed club, I will ask our esteemed commander to present the awards.'

From behind the mess settee, Manfred withdrew and presented our champions, each with one of their dress boots filled to the top with beer.

'It is tradition,' Manfred said to Charlie and Lothar, 'of

this motorcycle club, that every drop is drunk from these boots before any of us can leave.'

Charlie and Lothar looked at each other, sighed, and both took a gulp. Lothar took the floor, 'Now, you didn't say that we individually had to drink all the beer in our boots, so I think part of the tradition of this new motor-cycle racing club that seems to be hellbent on traditions, is that our erstwhile presenters, Kurt and Manfred should also partake of the famous boots!'

ON THE MORNING of the 21st, we took off into clearing skies. It was pretty bumpy up there, and much concentration was needed to just hold our formation. We spied a flight of lumbering BE2s, and Charlie signalled the attack. I felt the icy calm come over me as I pushed forward the throttle and put my beloved Albatross into a dive.

To my right was Charlie and, to his right, Lothar. We swept down upon the BE2s like avenging angels, with our guns spitting fury. We had taken them completely by surprise. I watched as my prey hurtled earthward.

Another aircraft, a little Nieuport that had joined the battle, crossed in front of me, stalking Charlie. I sent a burst from my machine-gun straight into it at very short range. It fell away with smoke trailing from its motor. I followed it down to see it crash into the ground. Another two had fallen to my guns.

I flew back to the airport landing behind the incoming red and black Albatross of Charlie. Lothar's bus was already parked. The tally was two to Charlie and one to Lothar. In just 20 minutes, the three of us had shot down five enemy aircraft!

The next day, reports came in of extensive RFC activity over the front. All Jastas were ordered up to block this air offensive.

Manfred led a small patrol of Charlie and myself. We spied four French Morane planes and a group of FE2bs. The latter aircraft was a slow pusher type aircraft.

Manfred signalled the chase. We slowly crept up on them and, when we were close enough, attacked from above. We each engaged with a different plane. I had the upper hand on my Fee, taking out the gunner first. Then giving the aircraft a long, raking burst to finish it.

Just as I saw the pilot slump, I heard the all too familiar sound of tracer ripping through my fuselage. I looked over my shoulder to see a French plane on my tail.

Something snapped. My icy calm was suddenly replaced with a berserk anger. I threw my crate into a spinning dive, luring the French Morane down in my wake, hoping he thought he had a hit.

Suddenly, I straightened out of the spin and threw my plane into a loop. Hanging upside down, I saw the French plane going past my guns, and I opened fire, then coming out on his tail, I continued to fire until he went down.

I straightened out close to the ground, shaken to the core by my berserk anger and action. I prided myself on my newly found calm demeanour, but it had certainly flown away today. I heard an aero-engine approaching from behind and breathed easier as Manfred slipped in beside me.

We landed in formation. Manfred jumped out of his

machine and ran across to me. He congratulated me on my two kills. Then noticing my anger, he put his arm around my shoulders, wordlessly expressing his understanding.

Manfred and Charlie had shot down their adversaries and had seen my first plane go down. Fearful that I had been hit, Manfred had followed me down and had witnessed the second kill. It was my 19th and 20th victory. Charlie had notched up his 22nd and Manfred his 46th.

It was also our 100th victory as a Jasta, a day we should have been celebrating, but Charlie hadn't returned. He would have been out of fuel by now, which meant one of three things. He had either force landed at another field, crashed somewhere or been shot down. My emotions now seemed rather paltry, with Charlie missing. While the entire German Army Aviation wing was informed of our great milestone, we were out searching, and on the telephone trying to locate Charlie.

At two o'clock in the morning, Charlie turned up with an army escort. Apparently, on his way home, he had spied a low-flying ground support aircraft and dived in to attack. Unfortunately, he was hit by British ground fire and was forced down between the lines. He abandoned the aircraft and headed for what he hoped was friendly territory. He eventually found some German troops in a dugout, and they guided him through a maze of artillery and trenches to a small village where his current escort had returned him to us. His uniform was covered in trench mud and he stunk of it, but he was a very welcome sight.

It was a very relieved bunch of fliers who crawled into their beds at 4am. The next day, Manfred and Lothar claimed their 47th and 10th victories, respectively.

Things were changing for our group. Charlie had shot down enough aircraft to be in line for the Knight's Cross and had been promoted to command Jasta 28. Manfred had been invited to dine with Kaiser Wilhelm in recognition of his outstanding leadership and our results. That would be followed by some leave.

I continued my letter to Maria.

'Dear Sweetheart, here I am again. The motorcycle races were fun, with Charlie and Lothar taking the honours. Since I last took pen to paper, I have claimed another four enemy aircraft. I had a moment after the fourth, but fortunately, Manfred was on hand to sort me out before I faced the others. It all faded instantly, though, when Charlie didn't return from the same mission. We all thought he had bought it, but he turned up early this morning without his plane and only a little bit the worse for wear.'

On April the 25th, my dear friend Charlie, in a new plane painted in his colours, thanks to Konnie's efforts, shot down two more enemy planes and saved Lothar from certain death. Rare for Lothar, he had been out manoeuvred and was taking some serious hits when Charlie slipped in behind the 'Fee' and shot it down.

Not so lucky was our good friend Sebastion. He was hit by British anti-aircraft ground fire and killed. Our 12–victory ace and dear friend to all of us had just been awarded the Cross of a Member with Swords. The cross was the second-highest bravery award for enlisted men and was very rarely awarded. He might have been a non–commissioned officer, but he was also a dear comrade. The whole Jasta was devastated.

The next day, Carl, Lothar and I avenged Sebastion's

death by each shooting down an enemy aircraft. It was my 21st victory, Lothar's 11th and Carl's 8th.

On the same day, the Kaiser ordered Jasta 11 to be changed to Jasta Ricthofen. It was so-called for three weeks before reverting to Jasta 11. Manfred never did say why he turned down such a high honour.

The same day as Charlie was departing to his new command, he received news that he had been awarded the Knight's Cross and the Pour le Mérite and I had been awarded the Knight's Cross. Both were high awards, and Manfred was very proud of us both. The Jasta Charlie was taking over was previously commanded by our old Commander Rudolf Lang. It had notched up two victories under his command.

It was great to see Charlie get his own command but sad to see him go. Sebastion dead, Charlie gone. Our tight-knit group was changing.

I continued my letter, bringing Maria up to date with all that had happened. It was a difficult passage to write. Here was Charlie with a new command, awarded the Pour le Mérite and the Knight's Cross. I'd been awarded the Knight's Cross, but on the other hand, our dear friend Sebastion was dead.

I finished my letter with the words: 'It seems that my world is one of great pride and great melancholy. Pride in what our Jasta is achieving, what I have achieved, but great sadness in losing dear friends. Forgive my ramblings, but I have so felt the need to express my thoughts and feelings. I know you will understand. I love you so very much. Yours in love, Kurt.'

On the 27th, we were back in the air. With a Knight's

Cross to my credit, I felt even more motivated than before. That morning, I shot down my 22nd victim and Lothar and Carl claimed their 12th and 9th victim, respectively. We were up against British Camels. They were nimble little fighters, and the torque of their engines meant they were very quick turning to the right but awfully slow turning to the left. We had noticed the pilots would often spin to the right to go left rather than make a slow turn, and they were quicker doing that. It gave us an edge knowing that, but they were still tough to deal with.

Our Jasta victories continued to climb the next day. Manfred claimed his 48th kill in the morning, and not to be outdone, I shot down my 23rd and 24th planes in the afternoon. I realised I had become an ice-cold efficient fighter pilot in the air. I didn't know whether I liked the feeling or not.

Oh, the fame that had come to our Jasta, particularly to us top-scoring pilots, was pretty heady stuff for the ego to handle. Still, balanced against that was the death and destruction one caused and the constant knowledge that the only thing that kept you alive was your own skill and a great deal of luck.

Every flight was a flight that you may not return from. It weighed heavily on all of us.

Manfred was determined to down his fiftieth victory before he met the Kaiser. On April the 29th, he got his wish.

Manfred led five of us on a patrol, and we were jumped by a trio of Spads. These were tough opposition, and these guys were after our blood. We squared off, and Manfred's adversary was the first to go down. I had my hands full, and after 10 minutes of throwing my beloved Albatross around the sky and taking lots of hits, I managed to get the upper hand and get a direct hit on the cockpit.

I saw the pilot slump and the Spad go into a death dive and crash. I was wrung out and too exhausted to feel any elation in winning. This had been my toughest victory by a long way, and it had taken every ounce of skill I possessed to come out on top. I was just very glad to have survived. Lothar had so shot up his quarry that it was forced to land on our side of the lines.

Up again in the afternoon, Manfred and I claimed our next two aircraft. It was Manfred's magical 50th and my 26th kill. This one felt like a walk in the park compared to the fight in the morning. There seemed to be a lot of novice British airmen flying at times.

Three hours later, Manfred and Lothar, flying together, did a repeat performance of Manfred and my earlier flight.

Just to top it off, in the early evening, Manfred brought down his fourth for the day, a much-vaunted British triplane. His skill and cunning in fights was becoming legendary not only on our own side but that of the British and French as well. We were also beginning to realise that our red aircraft were becoming well known to the enemy. The experienced enemy pilots sought us out, while the inexperienced would turn tail and race for home.

That night, the Jasta celebrated. A party had been planned as soon as the news of Manfred's leave had been announced. Carl and I had arranged for Maria and his fiancée, a nurse at the same hospital as Maria, to attend and bring some fellow nurses. Six of the girls managed to get time off and arrived by truck. Charlie flew back in, and several good friends of Manfred's turned up, including Werner Voss. I connected with Werner, and we managed quite a chat until the girls turned up.

When the girls arrived, Maria came straight up to me and gave me a long kiss and an even longer hug.

She whispered in my ear, 'I got your letter. You shouldn't have written all those details, but I'm glad you did. It helps me understand. I'm really proud of you.'

We hugged once more, then Charlie interrupted and demanded a hug from Maria.

It was a great night, and my fellow pilots were quite taken with my dear Maria. She was a good pianist and had a lovely singing voice. The other girls joined in, and a few beers and wines later, we were all in good voice.

After our guests had departed, we crawled into our beds, ready to face another day. The last day of April.

With Manfred leaving the next day, Lothar was made acting leader. Manfred had seen me earlier, saying it should have gone to me because of my victories, but the higher-ups wanted a von Ricthofen in charge. I didn't mind one bit. I considered Manfred and Lothar to be my very good friends and friends support each other, no matter what. On the last day of April, I shot down my 27th aircraft and Lothar his 16th.

What a month it had been. My total for the month was 22 aircraft, one better than Manfred's 21. There was no doubt that I would receive the Pour le Mérite very shortly.

In just four weeks, I had gone from a five–victory ace, really a 'nobody', to a genuine nationwide hero. Along with my friends, we had been photographed and featured in all the national newspapers. It was rumoured that they were even going to produce collectible photographic postcards of us.

It really felt crazy. It was very heady stuff, but what I really wanted now was some quiet time with my lovely Maria. Some time alone, where I could just be myself, and she could be just her lovely self. The party had not given us much time alone, and I was craving her company, her down to earth manner and her love.

CHAPTER 7

# Pour le Mérite, Promotion, Berlin

I COULD hear a voice in my head. It seemed to come from far, far away.' What happened next?' it asked.

Where was it coming from? Why was it becoming so insistent? Why wouldn't it go away? Why was it getting louder?

Why is it calling me? Why does the voice seem so familiar?

'I want you to come back to me; tell me what is happening?'

Suddenly, I knew where the voice was coming from. I thumped back into the chair, fully aware of my name, that the year was 1995, the month was September, and the day was the 15th.

Also, I was fully aware that I was in the middle of a past life regression because I also knew I was a pilot called Kurt, and it was the 1st day of May 1917. How could I be two people? How could I be feeling the emotions of both? How could I be in two places at once?

The voice asked me again,' What happened next?'

I started to tell him, and once again, I felt myself slipping completely into the life of Kurt. Manfred departed in a two-seater with my good friend Konnie piloting the plane.

Konstantin would carry on and have some leave. He had become the Jasta's technical officer, all of us being in awe of his engineering skills and his ability to quickly grasp anything to do with the technical designs and repairs of aircraft. He's mainly responsible for keeping our injured aircraft in the air. He's also an incredibly good pilot. We all feel safe being flown by Konnie.

After they left, Lothar organised a patrol, and as we flew, we soon spied a group of enemy planes below us. They were the much-vaunted Sopwith triplanes. In the ensuing dogfight, I brought down my 28th plane with my opening burst. Lothar got into a protracted fight, and as I circled around, I spotted a plane on Willi's tail. I closed in from the side and raked the plane. The pilot slumped, and the plane spiralled earthwards. Another plane spiralled past me, and I glanced up to see Lothar easing into formation beside me. He had just claimed his 17th kill. It was a good way to open our May scoring.

The same day I was awarded the Pour le Mérite.

I was the 18th aviator to receive the award. I also received a promotion, not in rank, but a command of my own Jasta. I was to take a week's leave on May 7th, then take over Jasta 29.

I had very mixed feelings. I loved Jasta 11 and my fellow pilots and was very proud of my achievements, but quite sad to be leaving.

My fellow pilots arranged a surprise party in my

honour, and to my great delight, Carl had arranged for his fiancée and my Maria to attend.

It was a great night. Charlie flew in, and to my great surprise, Werner Voss flew in to congratulate me. Lothar then read a letter addressed to me by his brother, Manfred.

'My dearest Kurt, little did I know when I first met you that you would become one of my greatest warriors and a very dear friend, not only to myself and Lothar, but to all the pilots of this Jasta. You have done us all proud, so my delicate little flower, you have developed some very sharp thorns. Congratulations on receiving the Pour le Mérite and command of Jasta 29.

'Oh, and by the way, you had better take that hideous coloured crate you fly with you. My warmest regards, Manfred.'

Lothar lifted his glass and toasted me, with everyone joining in. Maria then walked up to me and very publicly kissed me. Amid the cheers, I felt myself blushing to the roots.

'Speech, speech,' came the cry.

I stood amongst my fellow pilots.

'Ladies, gentlemen, if I may by a long stretch of imagination call my fellow pilots gentlemen, thank you for honouring me with this get-together. My time with Jasta 11 has been the most exciting and rewarding time of my life. We have an inspiring leader and friend.

'As a group, we have earned ourselves an enviable position in the German nation, and I know that more of you will join Manfred, Werner, Charlie and myself and will wear the Pour le Mérite in the near future. You have become the best friends that a man could ever wish to be amongst, and I will miss you all terribly, but I will follow your future efforts with great interest.

'To my Maria, I found you again on the way to join Jasta 11 and have come to love you dearly. You have inspired me to greater heights and have become the most important person in my life. Thank you.'

There was a moment's silence as I finished, and then Charlie and Werner hoisted me high on their shoulders, with Carl and Willi grabbing Maria and hoisting her on their shoulders. With much ado, cheers and laughter, they shouldered us in opposite directions around the mess before bringing us face to face.

With much laughter, my friends toasted us again. 'To the beautiful Maria and her delicate little flower.'

The evening descended into a right royal party, and I awoke late the next morning on the mess couch with Maria snuggled into me. Around the floor lay other pilots, no doubt where they had fallen. Carl was curled up on another couch with his fiancée. Some wag had found my nightcap and stuck it on my head during the festivities. There was obviously going to be no flying today.

Although I was supposed to go on leave on the 7th, I decided to do one last patrol with Jasta 11. Maria had leave starting the 8th, and we had decided to spend a week together in Berlin.

I took off with quite a large group on what was to be a successful day. Lothar opened the scoring with his 19th victim, and Carl claimed his 10th. Newcomer Otto downed his first enemy aircraft with Jasta 11, but it was not confirmed.

The evening patrol was to be my last with Jasta 11. It

was very cloudy with lots of mist in the air. The British were coming with their bombers intent on causing destruction. With their targets in mind, Lothar led us on the patrol once again. It was to be quite a patrol.

It wasn't long before we ran into ten SE5s that were soon joined by another six Spads. It became a melee amongst the clouds with individuals fighting individuals. I managed to get my sights on an SE5 and gave it a long blast. It spiralled earthwards with a black plume of smoke issuing from its engine. I saw it making for the British lines, so I assumed it made it home. Planes were falling in all directions, both ours and theirs. What the final outcome would be was anyone's guess.

Lothar was credited with shooting down the famous Captain Ball of 56 Squadron.

It had been an amazing last day for me, but now it was time to take a week with Maria, then assume command of Jasta 29.

I HAD ORDERED a first-class apartment on the train, so Maria and I were able to travel to Berlin in comparative comfort and privacy. It was a quiet and reflective time for us both. Maria had seen a lot of injuries and nursed a lot of soldiers and airmen.

It had been a sobering journey for her, and I admired her fortitude. For me, it had been a whirlwind of events, and I had been exceptionally lucky to come through it unscathed. I still mourned the loss of my good friend Sebastion, and even though it was only about four weeks since his death, it almost seemed a lifetime ago.

Time with Maria was to be prized. I was truly in love with my beautiful childhood friend. As the train lumbered on, she snuggled into my shoulder. I bent and kissed her hair. I was as content as a man could possibly be.

I raised her chin so that I could look into her beautiful blue eyes.

'Maria, will you marry me?'

She looked back at me. 'Of course, I will,' she replied. 'Now cuddle me some more.'

It was getting toward evening when we arrived in Berlin. I had booked us into separate rooms in a very flash hotel. As we walked in, I noticed people looking at us and whispering.

'Why are those people looking at us and whispering?' I asked Maria.

She smiled. 'Don't you know? she asked.

'I haven't a clue,' I replied.

'It's what's hanging around your throat that's creating the interest,' Maria replied. 'Come here over to the newsstand.'

Tugging me along, she moved to the newsstand that stood in the foyer and pulled out a paper.

'See, my darling, you are a national hero.'

I gasped as I took in the paper. A photo of myself was plastered across the front page of the paper. The write–up was a detailed account of my career with Jasta 11. I knew we had created a lot of interest as a group, but not as an individual.

'Leutnant Wolff, I am the manager of the hotel.'

A rotund man of middle age presented himself.

'We are honoured to have you stay with us. I have upgraded your rooms to our finest suite, and we have our finest booth set aside for you in our dining room. Please come with me. Our staff will take care of your bags.'

Somewhat bemused, I took Maria's arm, and we walked into the dining room. As we did, the civilian clientele stood and clapped us. I was terribly embarrassed and felt myself blushing.

Maria felt my discomfiture and squeezed my hand.

'Sweetheart,' she said to me, 'they need heroes in this war, and the Pour le Mérite makes you a public figure they can admire. Be proud, as I am of you.'

I smiled down at her. 'You make me much more proud than the Pour le Mérite ever will.'

The manager sat us down. 'Please, you are guests of the hotel. There will be no charge for you while you stay with us, and please select the best in wine and food. You have done us a great honour in choosing our hotel. I would only ask for an autographed photo.'

I accepted graciously, and when the photographer appeared as if by magic, I insisted that the manager sit with Maria and me in the photo shoot. He was delighted.

After dinner, we were escorted to the suite. There were adjoining rooms with huge double bedrooms and lounges attached. An interconnecting bathroom sat between the rooms. Both Maria and I were overwhelmed with the luxury.

The beds were four-posters, and the bath was huge and brimming with hot water.

'Who's for the first bath?' I cried.

Maria laughed.

'You go first, Kurt; you look exhausted.'

'Are you sure?' I asked.

Maria pushed me into the bathroom and closed the door.

'I'll hop in after you,' she called.

I stripped off my uniform and hung it on the clothes rack. I laid my Pour le Mérite gently on the seat and gently touched it with my fingertips. I still could not quite believe that I had succeeded in earning such a high honour and, in doing so, had become a national hero.

It seemed so surreal. Yet here we were. Flying with the nation's greatest hero, my good friend Charlie and I had also reached that point. Not only that, both Lothar, Carl and Otto were well on their way to joining us. It seemed like we had all gone from zero to hero in such a short time.

I stepped into the huge bath and lowered my body into the hot water. It was heavenly. I lay back and closed my eyes, letting the heat surround and comfort me.

I felt a disturbance in the water around my legs. I opened my eyes to the loveliest vision I had ever beheld. Maria was standing naked in my bath. My eyes travelled up her legs, pausing at the mysterious junction at the top of her legs. I felt an instant arousal as my eyes continued their journey across the flat plane of her stomach to the small, perfectly shaped breasts. Her nipples were standing large, and the ache in my groin intensified. Finally, my eyes came to rest on her exquisite face. Her smile was wide, and her eyes were sparkling with mischief and joy.

'Do you mind if I join you? After all, I did tell you I would hop in after you.'

Struck dumb, I nodded. She sank down into the bath facing me and, with a large cake of soap, started washing my chest. It was more than I could stand. I pulled her to me and kissed her with all the passion I possessed.

I felt her thighs wrapping around my legs, and there, in the bath, we consummated our love.

A fumbling first time for both of us but also an exquisite experience for both.

Afterwards, I lay back with Maria leaning back into me. My arms were around her, my hands perfectly cupping her breasts.

'Maria, I have never experienced anything so beautiful in my life. Thank you for sharing yourself with me.'

'Oh, Kurt, my sweetheart,' she murmured. 'The pleasure was not all yours. You have made me feel like the most beautiful woman in the world.'

I let my fingertips trace down over her stomach. 'To me, you are the most beautiful woman in the world, but why did you decide to give yourself to me tonight.'

'I promised you that we would lay together in a hotel bed, but you would have been too much of a gentleman to push your advantage,' she teased, 'and besides, making love for the first time in a bath just sounded heavenly, so I took a leap of faith and here we are. You don't think I am too forward, do you?'

I hugged her tighter and kissed her hair. 'Absolutely, you were forward, but thank God you were. You are quite right. I would have never pushed the advantage with you, not because I didn't want to. I did, but I thought I might offend you. Besides, I was quite timid. You are the first woman I have been with.'

Maria laughed merrily. 'Oh Kurt, you goose, you are the first man I have ever kissed and been with too, but I love you so much I just couldn't wait any longer to be with you.'

She turned, kneeling in front of me. 'Are you sure you are all right with us being lovers?'

I pulled myself into a kneeling position, facing her.

'Maria, it is more than all right. So much so that I would be honoured if you would consent to become my wife.'

Her eyes widened as she looked at me. I thought, 'Oh hell, I hope I haven't blown it.' She sat back on her haunches, still looking at me.

'You really mean it, don't you? You really want to marry me, don't you? Dear Kurt, you already asked me on the train, and I said yes then.'

'I wasn't sure you really realised because you were so sleepy.'

I nodded. 'But yes, I do, more than anything in my life. I want to share everything with you. I want to share ideas, I want to be able to talk as easily as we do, I want to love you as we have done, I want to raise a family with you, and I want to grow old with you. I know it is wartime, I know what I have to do is very dangerous, and there is every chance I may not survive the war, but I am willing to take the risk and fight for a life with you. It is easier for me, harder for you. So if you say no, I will understand. But if you say no, then I pray that we can stay friends and lovers because you are the light of my life.'

Maria stared at me for a few minutes, her normally sparkling eyes very blue and very solemn. She reached out a slim arm, her fingers tracing over my face.

'Kurt, my love, I hear what you are saying. If I were to lose you, it would hurt more than my life is worth, but I love you with all my heart and soul, and if I have to, I will hunt through all eternity to find you again.

'If we survive this war, then I would want to bear your children and, more than anything, grow old with you, so yes, I, too am willing to take the risk. So, my darling, with everything I am, I consent and would be honoured to be your wife.'

Kneeling in a lukewarm bath, we hugged each other, both happy beyond words. Eventually, we broke apart.

'Maria, would you mind if I shared your bed with you tonight?'

'I was rather hoping I could share yours,' she smiled impishly, 'but if you are so insistent, I am sure mine will suffice.'

With a new intimacy, we climbed into bed together. We made love again, then another two times after that.

The next day after arising late, we went down to the dining room for lunch, and after a time, we went for a walk in the streets of Berlin. It wasn't long before I spied a jeweller's shop, and I steered Maria toward it.

We asked to look at engagement rings, and we bought Maria a fine gold band mounted with three blue/black sapphires. It was a beautiful ring for my beautiful lady.

The rest of the week raced by in a blur of seeing the sights, making love and just being together. I was on cloud nine, and we were so enamoured with each other that other people almost seemed a hindrance.

The hotel manager was brilliant, making sure we had

the best of everything. We wanted for nothing. The week was like a calm in the middle of a storm.

All too soon, it was over. Maria was required back at the hospital, and it was time for me to assume command of Jasta 29.

We made a plan to coincide our time off. As commanding officer of a Jasta, I could, within reason, plan my time to suit Maria's days off, so she would work that out and send me her dates in a letter.

We both hoped it would work.

CHAPTER 8

# Jasta 29

I TOOK command of Jasta 29 on May 13th. On my first patrol, I led two of my new Jasta pilots along the lines. We spotted a flight of French Spads, and as we dived, I singled one out.

Coming out of the sun at them, my poor devil had little chance of getting away from my guns. I gave him a blast and followed him down to watch him crash. It was a momentous start for me and cemented my reputation amongst the pilots of my new Jasta.

On May 15th, I received a telephone call from Maria. It appeared my friends at Jasta 11 had been busy whilst Maria and I were in Berlin. On May 9th, Lothar had shot down his 21st plane, then on the 10th, both Lothar and Carl had claimed another apiece.

Lothar was also notified that he had been awarded the Knights Cross. On the 11th, Lothar claimed another, and Willi claimed his second. On the 13th, the same day as I claimed my victim, Carl and Lothar had claimed another apiece but had become separated during the fight.

Shortly after, Lothar was hit by ground fire as he crossed the lines. He was wounded in the hip. He landed in a field and lost consciousness, waking up in hospital with my dear Maria sitting beside his bed.

On the 14th, he learned he had been awarded the Pour le Mérite.

Carl had taken over as the Jasta leader, and Lothar was to be transferred to another hospital further behind the lines. So much had happened in such a short time. Maria urged me to visit Lothar if I could manage it.

I flew directly to Jasta 11's airfield and was met by Carl and Willi. We drove to the hospital, where we found Lothar in reasonable good cheer. We congratulated him on becoming the 20th recipient of the Pour le Mérite.

It was sad to see him being shipped off to another hospital. It would mean it would be some time before we saw him again.

As I got to grips with my new command, I was able to keep in touch with my friends from Jasta 11 via telephone calls from Carl. His successes continued, and by May 24th had shot down 17 aircraft. The same day, his brother Willi was shot in both knees but managed to land and was carted off to hospital.

The British now had a lot of the fearsome triplanes, and we were having a hard time contending with them. They had an awesome rate of climb and could out manoeuvre our trusty old Albatrosses. Manfred had shot down one of the first in April, and it had landed pretty well intact. Fokker had studied the plane, and rumours were rife that they were building us a triplane.

On the 25th and 26th of May, my dear friend Carl shot

down three planes taking his tally to 21. He was the fifth of our group to become a contender for the Pour le Mérite.

With the pilots of Jasta 29, I employed the same techniques that Manfred had used to train us. Charlie, Carl and I frequently corresponded, comparing notes and how we were each progressing with our new commands. We were all keen to carry on with the same vigour that Manfred had instilled within us.

On June 4th, Carl was awarded the Pour le Mérite. Charlie and I both made an unauthorised flight to Jasta 11 to congratulate Carl. The three of us had a great time catching up, and Charlie and I had time to talk to all our old comrades who were still on active service.

Long-time staffel member Georg had been shot down, but word had come through that he had been taken prisoner and was unharmed, and Otto had claimed another victim.

The next day, on June 5th, I received word that Charlie had been shot down and killed. I was shaken to the core.

Yes, I knew very well that with every flight, we all risked death, but Charlie was an extraordinary pilot and fighter. It seemed inconceivable that he had bought it, particularly as we had been joking together the previous day. His body had been recovered, and a state funeral was to be held in his hometown. I was able to get a day's leave to attend and flew down in my kite.

Manfred had stopped off for the funeral on his way back from leave. It was a sad occasion to catch up with Manfred, but nevertheless good to see him again. Manfred led the honour guard, which I was part of.

Catching up with Maria was proving difficult, so letters were being written every night to each other. We moved our base of operations on June 22nd. It was never that easy for the commander of a Jasta when these moves took place. You could guarantee a couple of days being grounded as you spent much time reorganising the staffel.

On the 25th, I received an exciting letter from Carl. When Manfred had returned, Carl had stepped down from the position of acting staffel leader as Manfred naturally resumed command. Carl's total was now at 28, but the great news was that a fighter wing of four Jastas had been formed with Manfred in overall command.

Carl had immediately been reinstated as staffel leader of Jasta 11 as Manfred stepped up. Our old friend Konnie had been promoted to technical officer of the whole fighter wing.

It was indeed exciting news, and I was quite envious of my friends' positions in the new fighter wing. I immediately made the time to put pen to paper and wrote back to Carl, congratulating him. I also took the liberty of mentioning that I would be keen to rejoin the wing if an opening should appear. I knew Carl would ensure that piece of the letter would reach Manfred.

On the 27th, I received news that we would again be relocating. Knowing that there would be no flying for a day or two, I determined to lead a patrol that afternoon. It wasn't long before I spied a Nieuport, and I felt the familiar icy calm settle over me.

I started to stalk the plane and, after 10 minutes, had closed enough to open fire. The Nieuport turned to fight, and the intricate aerial dogfight dance began, with each of us looking for the killing advantage. It didn't take too long for me to realise my skill was the better. I sent a lethal round into the plane and watched it spiral earthwards.

'That one was for you, Charlie,' I muttered to myself.

I brought my trusty old red and lime green Albatross down onto the grass for the last time at the current location and taxied to the line. As I climbed out of the cockpit, I was surprised to see another red Jasta 11 plane close by. I recognised Konstantin's crate by his crazy paint job. He appeared by my plane out of nowhere. I dropped down onto the grass beside him.

I knew without a shadow of a doubt that his news was bad.

Really bad. I looked at him.

'Who?'

'Carl. This morning.'

I sank to the ground, tears welling in my eyes. Konnie squatted beside me, laying a hand on my shoulder.

'We think he was hit by anti-aircraft fire. There were no planes near him, and he had turned off the petrol. He was gliding, then suddenly went into a dive. We are going out tonight to recover his body.'

He paused. 'I'm sorry, Kurt, I know you were very close to him.'

I nodded. 'Konnie, we are all so close in the Jasta 11 fraternity. It is so hard when we lose anyone.'

Konstantin nodded again.

I got to my feet. 'I am relocating Jasta 29 tomorrow. When is Carl's funeral? I would like to attend, as would Maria.'

'He will have a national funeral at St Joseph's in Courtrai in two days' time.

'Willi has requested that you and I attend as pallbearers. I have cleared leave for you, and I will make arrangements for Maria to attend.'

I put my arm around Konstantin's shoulder as we walked to the mess.

'Thank you, my friend. Are you going out in the retrieval party tonight?'

Konstantin nodded.

'I would come with you, but we have to organise things for the move tomorrow.'

Again, Konnie nodded. 'Your Jasta has to come first, Kurt.'

He paused, using my nickname.

'Wolfcub, I have talked to your staff here, and they have agreed to take some of the load off your hands.'

'Konstantin, you always look after us, don't you?'

He shook my hand as he returned to his kite. I watched him take off and then stood on the airfield as he disappeared from sight. I stood there for a long time, lost in my thoughts.

The funeral was again a sad affair. Manfred was in Hamburg visiting Lothar in Hospital. Otto was on leave and was to represent the staffel at the home service when Carl's body was transported home.

Willi had made the trip to Courtrai, wheelchair and all.

After the funeral, Maria and I spent some time with Willi and Konstantin. It was really nice to see my sweetheart in the flesh again. But sad as we three were the remaining originals of Jasta 11. Manfred and Lothar had come after us, but we were really missing them as well.

Two days later, I received transfer orders to command Jasta 11.

Two days after that, I reported to a newly returned Manfred.

# CHAPTER 9

# The Fighter Wing

**M**ANFRED came quickly around his desk and gave me a quick hug. 'Kurt, it is good to have you back in the team.'

He looked out the window at my old red and green Albatross.

'You still flying that old crate? Would you like a new one?'

I smiled. Manfred was on his fourth red Albatross.

I shook my head. 'No, my old crate is still doing fine, and I know all its idiosyncrasies now. I know exactly how it will react in any given situation, so I will keep my old crate. Besides, I am somewhat attached to it.'

Manfred slapped me on the back.

'Has your gear arrived yet?'

'No, I expect it later on today.'

'Good, get Konnie to show you your quarters and go reacquaint yourself with Jasta 11. You will find some old members from when you were here and of course some new pilots. They are all hand-selected, so hopefully will prove to be up to our standards. Don't worry about replacing Carl; everyone knows the history and friendships created in Jasta 11, and you will be made very welcome.'

I nodded my thanks and turned as Konstantin arrived at the door. As I went to leave, Manfred added, 'Oh, a meeting of all senior officers of the wing in two hours, here. That includes both of you.'

As I followed Konnie down the hallway, I commented, 'How the hell did you guys get such a palatial outfit?'

I had landed as directed at an estate of magnificent proportions. In fact, I had landed on the front lawn of a castle.

Konstantin laughed. 'The estate has been expropriated for military use, so welcome to the new home of our fighter wing. We moved in yesterday.'

We travelled up a broad stairway along a hall until Konnie stopped at a door. He swung it open.

'Your quarters.' He added, 'I am next door. I'm afraid we share the same bathroom.'

I looked into the room and gasped. A big four-poster dominated the room. It was luxurious.

'This is ridiculous,' I spluttered.

Konnie laughed. 'Get used to it, my dear friend, make the most of it. There is an interconnecting bathroom between our rooms.'

After checking out the rooms, we headed back downstairs to a huge lounge that had been turned into Jasta 11's mess. There, I met the new pilots and some of the old crew that I had known from when I was last with Jasta 11. Seven weeks with Jasta 29 had changed the makeup of Jasta 11.

I began to realise that seven weeks was a bit like a lifetime in the flying business. Many familiar faces had disappeared, and new faces had appeared. Suddenly I felt very old. I took an instant liking to one of the new pilots. His name was Willi. He was older and had served in the army before transferring to the air corp in 1915. He became a very good friend very quickly.

The estate was at Marke, just southwest of Courtrai. The good news was it was close to the hospital where Maria worked.

At the meeting, I got to meet the other Jasta Leaders and the adjutant. As I walked in, I spied Moritz, Manfred's wolfhound, asleep on the floor. He opened one lazy eye and looked directly at me. In a flash, he was on his feet with a joyous bark and tail going ninety to the dozen he was heading towards me.

I braced myself for the onslaught. Moritz was huge, and with apparent ease, he lengthened his body, placing his front paws on my shoulders. I knew what was coming as his great head neared my own.

Sure-enough, his big tongue was soon licking my face. As I disentangled myself from the dog, trying unsuccessfully to maintain some sense of decorum, I heard Manfred say, 'Gentlemen, this is our new commander of Jasta 11, Kurt Wolff. As you can see, Moritz thinks the world of him.'

'Damn dog.' I muttered as I shook hands with my fellow officers.

Jasta 4 was commanded by another Kurt, with three victories to his name, Jasta 6 by Eduard (12 victories) and Jasta 10 by Ernst. Like me, Ernst had just taken over command of Jasta 10. He wore the Knight's Cross, won in the infantry, and had earned the Pour le Mérite back in 1916 with eight victories. He was the eighth recipient of the Pour le Mérite and had a total of nine kills, the ninth also in July 1916. He had not shot down anything since. The adjutant's name was Karl. They were all older than me, and all oberleutnants. Konstantin and I were the junior officers present.

Manfred made the introductions, then asked us to take a seat.

Moritz, staying close to me, came and laid his great head on my lap. I absently scratched his head between his ears. He looked up at me with his great soulful eyes. I really did love that great hound of Manfred's, and I guess it was mutual.

The first thing Manfred did was announce that I had been awarded the Barvarian Military Merit Order with Swords.

I was somewhat taken aback as I had not been expecting any more awards.

Everyone present congratulated me, and it kind of levelled the playing field in terms of rank.

Manfred outlined the order of the Jastas. Eleven and Four were to be stationed on the estate, with Six and Ten at two separate but very close airfields.

We were given readiness take off rotations for each day's patrol. My flight would do the daybreak patrol followed by 10, 6, and then 4. The afternoon rota on was to be 10, 6 and 4, with my Jasta taking the last patrol of the day. Manfred would fly when he could and would move amongst the Jastas.

Flights would be of full Jasta strength and only authorised by Manfred, based on reports of enemy activity from the front line. This, Manfred believed, would increase our effectiveness, as we would be attacking known forces. The flights would go up in either Jasta flights or massed full wing flights, dependent on the number of enemy planes sighted. Manfred had a complicated telephone system set up where he could contact the four of us simultaneously.

Things were very hectic organisationally over the first few days. Our goal was made very clear. We were to rid the skies of fighters, trench strafers and bombers.

On July 4th, Manfred sent Jasta 4 toward Ypres, where activity was reported. By the time they arrived, the enemy planes had gone, so they returned to base. At 10.30 am, Manfred received more reports and led my flight to intercept the enemy.

It was great to be flying in station with Manfred again. Sitting in my old Albatross on such a still fine morning, just to the side and slightly aft of Manfred's red Albatross, brought back so many good memories for me.

On the way, we spied a flight of bombers. Manfred signalled the new target, and we swung in a large arc to cut off their retreat. The bombers turned to face us. With a massed 30 Albatross in the air, we had their measure. As we commenced the attack, four British triplanes joined in the fight. It was a right royal dogfight with planes flipping around all over the sky. My attention was taken up with an enemy in my sights. I fired the machine-gun taking out the pilot. It was my 32nd victory.

I swung my crate around, scanning the sky to see where the battle was progressing to. I could tell it was petering out.

I glanced earthwards and, to my horror, saw Manfred's

red plane heading down in a dive. Two other Albatross dived away after it. One I recognised as Otto's. The planes straightened out, and I could see them land in a paddock by some troops. I swooped down over the field. There wasn't room for me to drop my kite down.

Otto and the other pilot had dashed to Manfred's plane and climbed up on the wing. As I circled about 100 feet off the deck, I watched them lift Manfred out of the cockpit. He was obviously wounded. Otto gave me a reassuring wave.

I set course for the airfield, landing quickly. I dashed into the chateau, raising the alarm. I phoned the hospital, alerting them to Manfred's whereabouts so an ambulance could be dispatched. I knew Otto would remain with him to that point. The two other staffel leaders of Four and Six and I joined the adjutant, Karl, and grabbed a car and raced to the hospital at Courtrai.

We were lucky to time our arrival as the field ambulance arrived. Manfred was still conscious but in great pain from a head wound. The hospital staff rushed him inside.

We waited nervously while the doctors and nursing staff worked on Manfred. He had been wounded in the head, but we didn't know how bad it was. In the afternoon, he was declared out of danger and able to receive visitors. His head was heavily bandaged, and he looked pale and weak. It was a shock to us all, but he promised us he would soon be back in service.

Kurt was appointed acting wing commander while Manfred was in hospital. Konnie and I flew a two-seater out to where Manfred had force landed and checked his red

Albatross out. Konnie did a few quick repairs, and I flew it back to base.

The next morning dawned clear, and Kurt led a flight of a dozen planes from across the Jastas. Flying in formation, I spotted two Albatross engaged with two Sopwith two-seaters and six triplanes.

I blipped my throttle to attract Kurt's attention. As he looked across at me, I indicated the fight. He nodded, and we dived down to fight, with the others following. I attacked and chased a triplane southwards, finally shooting it down to claim my 33rd victory.

Upon landing, I found the flight had claimed a total of three triplanes. That afternoon, the wing shot down another six planes, making nine kills for the day. Our only casualty was Kurt, who had received a slight injury when his engine cut out and he forced landed.

Bad weather hampered flying over the next three days, so I borrowed a car and set off to Courtrai with the hope of catching up with both Manfred and Maria.

As I walked in to see Manfred, I found Maria clearing away his lunch. I stole a quick kiss, and she promised to see me when she came off duty at 3.00pm. I sat down with Manfred and described our successes as a wing on the seventh. It cheered him up immensely.

At three, I caught up with Maria, and we walked to a café and ordered dinner.

As she sat down, she looked across at me as I took my seat.

'I have so missed you, Kurt. It is really nice just to have some time on our own.'

A waiter brought a menu, and once he had gone, I

stretched my hand across the table, gently squeezing her hand. 'I have missed you too, sweetheart. Maybe we can organise some time together now that I am so close.'

'That would be really nice, but I've got a short leave, and Papa has just arrived, so I will need to spend some time with him.' she replied.

As she looked at me, her eyes widened.

'Kurt! You have got another medal! You didn't tell me,' she cried indignantly.

I felt myself blushing.

'I only heard about it the day I joined the fighter wing, and I only received it yesterday. It's not that important. My Knight's Cross has a higher standing.'

'I don't care. I want to know all about it and what it is for,' replied Maria.

'It is The Barvarian Military Merit Order with Swords, and it is for valour.'

She smiled,' Do you remember when we met on the train, and you didn't think much of yourself because you had not shot down a plane?'

I nodded.

'Do you remember what I told you?'

Again I nodded.

'Well, see, I was right, wasn't I? You have shot down planes. You have earned your medals and are now a bona fide national hero. I am so proud of you.'

I smiled, 'Thank you, Maria. You know it is a little scary being in this position. Everyone expects great things of you.'

'Oh, Kurt, you have earned your accolades. You don't have to keep earning them. Now, let's eat.'

'That may be so, but I still need to inspire my pilots.' I

replied. 'Now I would really like to catch up with your Papa. Where are you going to be staying?

Maria gave me the address of the hotel.

I walked Maria back to her quarters after dinner and motored back to the airfield.

The next day dawned clear, and by mid-morning, I was leading a patrol toward Ypres.

Suddenly we were taken unawares by a dozen or so triplanes.

They came at us from out of the sun with all guns blazing. I turned towards them and opened fire. It was like being caught in a hornet's nest. I rolled and looped and dove, trying desperately to avoid their guns and at the same time draw a bead on someone.

Suddenly, I felt a ripping pain in my shoulder and left hand. A row of bullets struck my plane and knocked out my machine-gun. Now, I was unarmed and injured. With my good hand, I thrust forward the stick and put my bird into a steep dive. The pain was really escalating now. I thought I had taken bullets in the left shoulder and hand.

I pulled out of the dive at 500 feet, hoping no one had followed me down. All was quiet, so I looked for a place to land before I passed out.

The only flat place seemed to be alongside the railway track. I eased my kite down. This was going to be difficult. The Albatross was a difficult plane to land at the best of times. One-handed wasn't going to be pretty. Gently I eased my crate down and throttled off.

Just as the wheels were getting close to the ground, a gust of wind sent me sideways, and my wheels touched down on the railway itself. There was a resounding crash as the undercart was ripped off, and my plane upended itself. I came to rest hanging from my straps.

Infantrymen had seen the crash and were by my side almost instantly. They lowered me out of the aircraft and gently carried me to a truck, and loaded me in the back.

I must have lost consciousness because the next thing I knew, I was being carried into the hospital. The wound in the shoulder was fortunately just a flesh wound, but a machine-gun bullet had gone clean through my left hand. It looked like I was going to be out of action for a while. I must have passed out again while they were tending my wounds. I woke up in a hospital bed.

Sitting at my bedside was Konnie. I could hear voices. I turned my head. Konstantin was talking to Willi and Otto, who were sitting at the end of the bed. Manfred's voice broke through my head. My eyes must have looked puzzled.

Konnie spoke, 'Kurt, you are in hospital and are sharing a room with Manfred. You were shot down and apparently crash-landed. You have a slight wound in the left shoulder and have taken a bullet through your left hand. It will take a little while to heal. Otto and Willi and I have come to see how you are and brought you some clothes and nightwear.'

I turned to my friends. 'What happened to my kite?'

Manfred smiled from his bed. 'You completely wrecked it, Wolfcub, so now you will have to let me get you a new one.'

Konstantin joined in, 'Willi and I had a look at it on the way over. Even with my great technical skills, it would be impossible to rebuild. Let's face it. You demolished the undercart, the prop and the top wing. The fuselage looks like someone took to it with a battering ram. Then there's twenty–five bullet holes and a smashed machine-gun,' he grinned. 'So, Manfred's right, we can, at last, get rid of that terrible paint job you have been flying.'

I grimaced with pain, then replied, 'But I like my paint job.'

My friends laughed. I could tell they were mighty relieved that I had got down more or less in one piece and was out of danger.

Konnie pulled out my nightcap and gave it to me. 'I thought you always flew with this ridiculous cap in your pocket. I found it on the floor of your room.'

'I always fly with it. Maybe it fell out of my pocket.'

'Well, don't tell Maria,' came Manfred's voice, 'If she finds out, she'll likely kill you,' he joked. 'Now, gentlemen, we need to get serious. Willi, I want you to be acting staffel leader while Kurt is out of action, and I want Kurt von Doring and all of you to report to us each day and keep us up to speed with what's happening with the wing.'

The three airmen nodded, then, seeing how tired both Manfred and I were, made their excuses and left.

The matron of the hospital arrived with a nurse.

'Kurt, this is Kate, she has already been assigned to Manfred, and she will also look after your wounds. I have assigned Maria to help when she returns from her leave, and she will be organising your food and changing your bedpans.'

She gave me a long slow wink as she mentioned the latter, and I blushed bright red.

The matron wasn't such a dry old stick. In fact, she had a wicked sense of humour. That night I wrote a letter to Maria explaining what had happened.

I awoke the next morning to find Maria at my bedside.

She propped my pillows and made me more comfortable while Kate examined my wounds.

'We will redress them every day Kurt, as we do with the Captain over there. I hope you don't squeal as much as him.'

Manfred gave Kate a dirty look.

'Don't believe anything she says,' snapped Manfred, 'she is just a bossy young lady.'

Kate stalked over to Manfred's bed.

'Call me that again, and you will go without dinner, you, you, stubborn goat!'

With that, she stalked out of the room.

Maria's gentle laugh caressed the room. I looked at her.

'Did I just miss something?'

Her eyes twinkled. 'Oh, Yes. Kate really likes Manfred, and Manfred really likes Kate, but both are too stubborn to admit it, so they spar verbally every day. The whole hospital staff are running bets on how long they can keep the pretence up.'

I looked across at Manfred. He was blushing and pretending to ignore Maria. I had never seen Manfred blush or look so uncomfortable.

'You know, Maria, I believe you may be right. The boss is in love. Wait until I tell our fellow pilots,' I teased.

Manfred glared at me.

'Do that, and I'll bust you down to sergeant,' he threatened.

I laughed. At least it wouldn't be totally boring in hospital, Maria tucked my wounded paw in carefully, and I snuggled down for my second night in hospital.

# CHAPTER 10

# Out of Action

I WAS BORED, irritable, sore and just plain miserable. It was the end of the first week. I was among the walking wounded, so was able to walk the grounds with Maria when she was off duty. I looked forward to those times, but they were few and far between. Her papa had visited me before heading back home.

It was great to catch up with the vicar again, and I was able to ask him formally for Maria's hand in marriage.

Manfred and I both worried incessantly about Jasta 11 and the group. Manfred's worries were bigger than mine, as his senior officer, who had been appointed to run the fighter wing in Manfred's absence was interfering in the running of the group while Manfred was out of action. He would get very angry and developed an intense dislike of the man.

The senior officer commanding ordered Kurt von Doring to barricade the air. He wasn't concerned about shooting planes down. Manfred and I knew he was totally out of touch with the real war in the air and how it should be conducted. Manfred sent a flurry of letters off to any influential person he knew who could intercede in the shambolic state of affairs.

During the week, Maria got news that her papa had become ill on his journey home and got leave to attend him. She didn't want to go but knew she had to.

The day after she had departed, Manfred and I were picked up by Manfred's father and driven by car back to our base. We had a day pass and were only able to take the trip if a nurse accompanied us.

The obvious choice was Kate. The car trip was fun. We were recognised by marching troops and hailed by them all the way. It was great to catch up with the group again. Back at hospital, two days later, on a heavily overcast day, half the pilots from the wing decided to visit us. There were so many that Kate ordered all of us out onto the hospital steps for visiting hours!

A week later, Manfred was released from hospital with strict instructions to run the fighter group in his own efficient way, but on no account was he cleared to fly again. The senior officer that had caused so much mischief was reassigned to the eastern front.

On his return, Manfred found out that the new Fokker triplanes were very close, and his fighter group would be the first recipients. He was told it could outfly and outclimb anything the British could put up. He phoned me at the hospital to pass on the news.

The following day he rang to tell me that Otto had been killed.

Just two days earlier, he had shot down a British

triplane and was in contention for a Pour le Mérite. I was very sad for he had become a great friend.

I was exceedingly keen to get back to Jasta 11. So much action was taking place that I felt I needed to be there. Even if I was ground-based.

On July 30th, Jasta 10 Commander was replaced by Werner Voss. Werner had the same amount of kills as me and carried the same tin wear. He would surely make a difference to Jasta 10, which was the lowest-scoring Jasta in the group.

I managed to escape hospital and return to the airbase on August 7th. Like Manfred, I was forbidden to fly.

Maria had returned with the news that she would have to quit the hospital and return home to look after her father. She would leave in a week's time. Kate and Maria had a two-day pass, so commandeered a car and drove me to our headquarters. It was great timing as Jasta 6 leader Eduard had just been awarded the Pour le Mérite, and the fighter group were having a celebration in his honour.

I enjoyed the party and really enjoyed having Maria on my arm. Manfred was very careful to keep Kate on his arm, leaving no doubt in his pilots' minds that Kate was forbidden to them. Eduard's medal had not arrived, so Manfred slipped his own off and gave it to Eduard for the night.

The following day, an order came to recycle our Albatross back to the factory for overhauling. Command of Jasta 11 was to stay with Willi until I was cleared. However, despite being forbidden to fly missions, I managed to talk Manfred into letting me help Konnie organise the ferrying of the Albatross back to the factory and flying them back to the airfield. This way, I could fly again without really defying orders.

I said a sad farewell to Maria and asked her to give my love to her father and my aunt and uncle.

Three days after returning, our airfield was bombed. The same day Werner brought down his 35th plane. The next day saw lots of group action, and Jasta 11 pilot Hans Wolff was wounded. Hans was not related to me and had only recently joined my staffel.

Both Manfred and I were starting to fret about being left out of combat.

The action was fierce, and our group gained more kills, but we were also losing good men. By August 16th, Manfred had had enough. Taking to the air in his red Albatross after 40 days' absence, Manfred spotted a Nieuport and shot it down, claiming his 58th victory. His landing looked pretty hairy when he came in, so I ran over to his plane. He was all in.

'Kurt, my head is throbbing. I don't think I can get out by myself.'

I knew that Manfred was still troubled by the bad headaches that he had experienced in hospital.

'Come on, old friend,' I said, 'let me help you.'

I eased him up out of the cockpit, down onto the lower wing, and onto the ground. Konnie and Willi had arrived by now. They summoned a stretcher, and we carried Manfred to his bedroom and told him to stay put and go to sleep. It was the only time he ever took or obeyed an order from Konnie, Willi and myself.

That night and the next morning, we were bombed again.

I was getting a bit teed off with this bombing lark.

The next day one of our new Jasta 11 pilots shot down his first enemy plane. It was Jasta 11's 200th victory. I was very proud of my Jasta.

Manfred decreed a large victory party was in order, and the chateau was transformed into a party house. Invitations were sent to all off-duty nurses at the hospital to attend. It went without saying that Kate was included. Even if she was on duty, the matron would change her roster so that the girl of the nation's greatest hero could be on his arm. The matron wasn't slow. Photographs were always taken at these events, and they promoted her hospital wonderfully.

It was another wonderful party, and with plenty of women to go around, the pilots were trying to outdo themselves in gallantry. I spent a good part of the evening laughing very hard at their antics, but I really missed my Maria.

The following day, Manfred was cautioned not to fly again until the last traces of his wound had disappeared, then only to fly when absolutely necessary.

His day was improved when Eduard shot down his 26th plane.

On the same evening, we got warning of British bombers heading our way. Within minutes we were all outside holding rifles. We had set up a machine-gun on the front lawn, which I immediately commandeered. In the distance, we picked up the drone of aircraft engines.

As they grew louder, Manfred called out, 'Here they come, let's give them a warm reception.'

The bombers came in a single line over our base, with most of the bombs dropping harmlessly on the airfield.

We gave them a hot reception, with the third aircraft taking a direct hit from my machine-gun.

Smoke started to pour out of the engine. There was a distinctive crack from Manfred's sporting rifle as he fired, and we all saw the pilot slump. The plane was trailing smoke and descending past the airfield, suddenly plummeted to the ground.

The fourth bomber aborted its attack and headed off in another direction.

Three days later, Eduard was killed in combat. When he failed to return, Manfred sent out several planes to look for him.

Later we received a report that had come in from the British about a downed German plane. He had crashed right on the forward lines. He was buried where he crashed. All of us were deeply saddened by Eduard's death. Again, it brought home to me how fragile our lives were.

Manfred approached me and said, 'I have been requested to go and check out the prototype Fokker triplanes tomorrow. Konnie is going to fly me there. Want to come?'

I grinned, 'Count me in. I would love to see them.'

The next morning Manfred and I squeezed into the rear cockpit of a two-seater and, with Konnie at the controls, flew to the Fokker factory. There we admired the new triplanes and spoke at length to Antony Fokker.

We flew back to base with a great deal of excitement. The triplane was a real looker and if it performed like they said, it would be a great addition to our Jastas.

# CHAPTER 11

*The triplanes*

M ANFRED had taken his red bird up again and, during his patrol, had claimed his 59th victim. He again was pretty exhausted and went straight to bed.

The next day, there was great excitement when two of the new Fokker triplanes arrived.

All the pilots trooped down for a look. They had been allocated to Werner and Manfred as they, along with Konnie and me, had been to the factory and were most familiar with them. Both were prototypes being number 102 and 103. Manfred took number two and Werner number three.

Manfred was too tired to try his out, so Werner took off and flew around the airfield.

We watched from the ground as he put it through its paces. The rate of climb was incredible, and aerobatically it was superb. Watching from the ground, I could feel my excitement rising. With this machine, we would be more than on an even footing with anything the enemy had.

Werner touched down, and we crowded around as he gave his verdict. He was ecstatic.

'It performs so well. It climbs like nothing on earth, and you can almost throw it around with abandon. It is so manoeuvrable,' he enthused.

Manfred turned to me.' How is the hand, Wolfcub?'

'Pretty good,' I replied.

'Think you could handle a circuit in the triplane?'

I grinned. 'Really?' I flexed my hand. 'I'm sure I can wrap it around a joystick.'

'Well, we are going to be sharing 102 when you are officially back on deck, so you may as well have an unofficial flight now. Werner, talk Kurt through the idiosyncrasies of the planes, then take off with him.'

Werner walked to the plane with me and helped me with the belt.

'Now remember, Kurt, she will take off in a shorter distance because of the extra lift from that third wing, and her rate of climb is much faster than the Albatross. Likewise, you will find your turn rate much quicker. Follow me up and do as I do.'

He patted me on the shoulder and ran across to his triplane.

Werner was quite right. As I followed him down the airstrip, the tail lifted very quickly.

As he eased back on the stick, I followed suit.

I couldn't believe it. The bird just soared. It made the Albatross feel like a flying brick. I was elated.

Within 15 minutes, following Werner through a series of manoeuvers, I had tried out most of the aircraft's limits and was feeling very comfortable with it. Werner flew alongside and pointed down at the airfield where the pilots and ground staff were still watching. He held up his hand, pointing to himself and then to me. He then indicated a loop and held up five fingers.

I pointed down to the ground and then replied with five fingers, did the loop with my hand and pointed at us both, indicating I had understood.

We both grinned like naughty schoolboys and put our planes into a dive towards the airfield. We held formation about thirty feet apart and directly over the airfield at 500 feet, we pulled back on the sticks, both executing a perfect loop while still holding formation. We brought the planes in to land, still holding formation.

Our fellow pilots were clapping and laughing as we stopped and climbed out of our machines.

Manfred called out to us, with a slight grin twitching his lips.

'You call yourselves staffel leaders and pull stunts like that? More like American cowboys if you ask me!'

Werner and I were both so excited about the triplanes that our enthusiasm soon spread to the rest of the pilots. Everyone was excited about the new planes and looking forward to when the whole group was flying them.

The next few days were very frustrating for me. I was still officially unable to fly. It was still a painful stretch of my hand to operate the machine-gun, so I was just going to have to be patient. Manfred sent me on leave, so I travelled to my home town and caught up with my auntie and uncle and Maria and her papa. Her father was much improved.

I stayed a couple of nights with my aunt and uncle and a few nights at the vicar's place. He had placed me in a room next to Maria's, and an hour or two after bedtime, I felt a presence beside my bed.

'It is me, Kurt,' murmured Maria. I felt her lift the blankets and climb in beside me.

She snuggled in, and we lay in each other's arms, just enjoying the intimacy of the moment. A little later, we became more amorous and quietly made love, then talked until the wee hours of the morning. It was the most beautiful time of my life, as was the following week.

Every night Maria would appear after lights out and crawl into my bed. It was a week of delightful intimacy. Some nights we made love; some nights, we just talked and snuggled together, enjoying the closeness.

During the day, my cousins Helga and Frieda would sometimes turn up, and the four of us would enjoy the friendships that had developed throughout our lives. I couldn't have asked for more from my leave. On the last night, the vicar, with just my Aunty and Uncle and cousins present, performed a quiet marriage ceremony for Maria and me. We decided to keep it quiet as marriage for pilots was not encouraged.

Manfred had four weeks' leave coming up and had invited me to stay for the last two days of my leave. It was a substantial honour to be invited to the Ricthofen home, so I packed my bags and said goodbye to my family and my darling Maria, and caught the train to see my good friends Manfred and Lothar.

The days spent with the Ricthoftens went very quickly. They were a delightful family and made me feel very welcome. Lothar and I were able to have some good chats. He was due back to the Jasta on September 25th.

I had been cleared for return to duty on the 11th and would resume command of Jasta 11. Manfred updated me on the group. He had claimed his 60th and 61st kill in the new triplane, and Werner had claimed his 40th. Willi had been wounded but would recover.

It seemed Werner was going crazy in his new triplane and had claimed more kills, but Manfred was unsure of how many. The three of us talked at length about the attributes of the new triplanes. Lothar was anxious to get back and try one out after hearing our stories.

The next day I took the train back to base arriving on the 11th.

Konstantin bought me some mail on the 12th. There was a letter from Maria and a letter with the royal crest on the envelope. I tore it open and found to my surprise, a personal letter from the Kaiser approving my promotion to oberleutnant.

Konstantin was the first to congratulate me.

That night I sat down and wrote to my Maria.

'My darling Maria, I have received a promotion to oberleutnant, authorised by the Kaiser himself. I have been so honoured over the last few months that I find it hard to believe what has happened to me. I feel that I must persevere in my efforts to down enemy aircraft to justify everyone's belief in me. In the last battles, I have engaged with more than twenty Englishmen without success. Maybe the triplane will give me the advantage I need. I miss you very much. Thank you for loving me. I will love you forever. All my love, Kurt.'

I gave the letter to the adjutant to post, then set off to find eight pilots of Jasta 11 for the late afternoon patrol. I intended to fly the triplane, as my old Albatross had not been replaced. Besides, with Manfred away, it was always going to be the plane I flew. It was a bird. I really loved it.

I had found to my delight I could put it accurately wherever I wanted. The more I flew it, the better I liked it.

# CHAPTER 12

# Life, Death and Life

## SEPTEMBER 15TH, 1917

A T 4.30PM, I lifted off in the triplane. Behind me, eight of my Jasta 11 comrades in their Albatross followed. My wingman took station off to the left of me. I glanced skyward. It was very overcast with lots of rolling cloud. Not great flying conditions. We would be lucky if we could all stay together and not get lost.

We climbed towards the front. At 8,000 feet, we entered heavy cloud. Pretty much blinded by the cloud, I kept climbing, the damp vapourous cloud wisping around me like a mist in the open cockpit.

At 9,000 feet, I popped out into clear. My wingman popped out about 200 feet off my left wingtip. I looked around.

We had lost the other seven.

I altered my course with my wingman holding position. Soon the skies started to clear a bit. The skies were empty. We flew on as the watery sun started to emerge.

At 10,000 feet, it was cold as hell, but I could see planes appearing out of the murk. I could see the rest of my Jasta, about 1,000 feet lower than me and several miles away.

They were falling onto some enemy planes at about 7,000 feet. Between them, I spied a flight of bombers with an escort of eight Sopwith Camels. As I watched, four of the Sopwith fighters broke away and dived on our comrades. I glanced around the sky; we were by ourselves and had the sun and height advantage. I signalled my companion, and we stealthily made our approach toward the remaining four Sopwith Camel fighters and the bombers. If we could deal with the agile Camels, the bombers would be easy meat.

As we arrived above them, I signalled my intentions to my wingman.

Pushing the triplane into a dive, I lined up on a Camel, raking its tail with machine-gun fire.

As I rocketed past, I hauled back on the stick and threw it into a steep banking turn, at the same time climbing rapidly using the triplane's superior climbing rate to get above the Camels and gain an advantage.

I glanced across the sky and saw that my companion was fully engaged with an enemy plane. I lined up on the second plane, raking him with my machine-gun. The third Camel put a burst through my tail. I hauled back on the stick, climbing away. I threw the tripe into a hard–right turn and came back at the Camel spitting bullets.

I now had three of the Camels on me. I threw a loop and came down directly behind one giving it a peppered fuselage. Straight away, I went into a skidding left-hand turn to face an oncoming Camel.

It dived below me, and I threw the plane into another loop. Rolling out on top, I put her into a dive, firing at the same plane now below me.

Suddenly, above the sound of my engine and my chattering machine-gun, I heard a sharp cracking sound. I glanced up and, to my shock, saw that the top wing had movement on the leading edge. I could see a lot of movement around one of the struts.

I knew I was in serious trouble.

I throttled back. Time slowed. How was I going to extract myself?

At 9,000 feet with three Camels fighting me, the odds had suddenly lengthened. Suddenly, a welter of machine-gun bullets ripped through the fuselage and cockpit and engine area.

I felt the excruciating pain as one passed through my body. Momentarily, I blacked out. I came to realising I was in a death dive toward the ground. Flames were coming from the engine. With great effort, I switched the engine and petrol off.

Thank God. The flames vanished.

I was hurting now. Really hurting.

I eased the stick back, gently flattening out the dive. Through the pain, I came to the realisation that the tripe's top wing had an inherent weakness. I had to get down and tell Manfred. The altimeter showed 2,000 feet. It had been a long dive. I was surprised the top wing had held together during the dive.

I looked down at the ground. I was above the trenches, and a ground attack was underway.

Everywhere I could see soldiers falling and hear the rattle of gunfire.

A great melancholy settled over me. Tears began to trickle down my cheeks.

For the first time in my life, I thought,' What are we doing? We are killing each other. For what?'

Wearily and with great effort, I raised my hand and pushed my goggles up. My altimeter showed just 1,500 feet. The top wing was really flapping around now.

Ahead I could see a paddock just behind our lines. I thought, 'If I could just get there.'

With the last of my strength, I hauled the aircraft onto a heading that lined me up for a final approach. I could hear the sound of ground battle below as the air hummed around the wings as I glided on.

The pain was now intense. I thought of my dear Maria. Would I ever see her again? Oh, how I loved her! Then, in the distance, I heard a strange voice calling me.

'Can you hear me? I want you to abandon the plane and come back to me.'

'What?' I mumbled.

I could see the paddock. The altimeter was at 200 feet.

With what seemed a great effort, I lined the aircraft up for a final approach.

The voice again penetrated my subconscious, 'It is imperative that you come out of the plane. This is Dennis. Please abandon the plane.'

I took my last breath and gently passed over. I was outside the plane now, but I could still see myself in the cockpit. What on earth was going on? I watched as the tripe nosed into a slight dive and crashed into the ground. The top wing crumpled forward. I realised that no one would be able to detect the fault. Soldiers ran toward the wreck and gently lifted me out.

'He's a goner,' said one soldier.

An officer strode up and looked at me.

'Dead. Looks like he took a bullet through his chest.'

He undid my helmet.

'God, it's one of Ricthofen's best. I recognise him from newspaper photos. Gently now, lads.'

I watched in consternation as they carried me away. What was going on? Then and only then came the realisation that I had been killed.

I was dead.

So, how could I still be thinking?

From a distance, the insistent voice reached me, 'I want you to return to me. This is Dennis. You are in hypnosis, and I want you to move away from the life you are experiencing.'

I turned away from the scene of my aircraft. In front of me stood my friends, Carl, Charlie, Sebastion and Otto. The two Eduards were there, as were other members of Jasta 11.

All my dead friends and comrades gathered around me. I could feel their energy.

I turned back in time to watch my funeral. Maria and her father were there.

'Oh, God, Maria!'

She was looking right at me but not seeing me. Tears were running freely down her cheeks. She said quietly. 'I will find you, my love. I will find you again even if it takes me all eternity.'

I moved closer, and she looked into my eyes but could not see me.

'I feel you. Kurt, I know your spirit is right beside me. I love you, and I swear I will find you again.'

I felt incredibly sad. It was going to be a long time without Maria. I looked at my pallbearers. Willi and Konstantin were there along with Werner. I watched as one of my comrades handed my medals, displayed on a black velvet cushion, to Maria.

'I can't see Manfred or Lothar?' Charlie redirected my gaze. Lothar and Manfred were in the parlour of their parent's home. Lothar was gazing with far-seeing eyes out the window. Tears were trickling down his cheeks. Manfred sat with his head in his hands. A telegram was open on the table. Moritz was by his side whimpering.

Carl said, 'They have just heard, my dear friend.'

Again, I heard the strange voice.

'I want you to walk through the door and come back to this life.'

Charlie turned to me, 'It's time to go, Wolfcub.'

He indicated a door.

'Go where?' I questioned in a panicky voice.

'Back to the life you came from,' replied Charlie.

'Pass through the door, and it will all come back to you,' said Carl.

I seemed to be being pulled to the door.

Sebastion called, 'Remember us all and the time we had, the dear friendships we had. We will all meet again sometime in another life. Goodbye, my friend.'

I passed through the door, and as I did, I recalled my

current life, and yet the memories of this experience were so very real.

I heard the voice of Dennis calling me. I travelled toward the voice. I felt myself becoming aware of my existing body.

Dennis was calling me through my current life as a baby, a little boy, a teenager, a young man. Suddenly I stopped.

Dennis questioned me, 'You have stopped moving forward. Where are you?'

'I am at my wedding,' I replied.

'What year are you in?' he asked.

'1976.'

'What is significant? Do you recognise anyone from the life me you have just experienced?' asked Dennis.

'Maria. Maria is my bride. She has found me.'

Tears ran unheeded down my cheeks.

'Dennis said, 'I want you to travel forward in time now to the present day. As you do, you will become calm and relaxed. You will remember in vivid detail the life you have described to us but will remain calmly detached from it and be very much in the here and now.

'The experience will remain a very positive one for the rest of your current life.

'I will now count you up to three.

'One, feeling relaxed and calm and very positive about your experience as your trance begins to lighten.

'Two, feeling really good about the whole experience and quite enlightened as you become much more aware of your surroundings.

'Three, feeling wonderful, happy and at peace with yourself. Open your eyes now!'

I opened my eyes. Tears were still flowing down my cheeks, but here I was sitting in a chair, looking at my classmates.

I was back in September 1995.

\* \* \*

*September 15th, 1995*

I FELT exhausted, both emotionally and physically. I was wrung out. Tears still trickled down my face.

Dennis spoke, 'how are you feeling?'

'Absolutely shattered,' I replied, then added, 'But I would not have missed that for the world.'

'How much of it do you remember?'

'All of it with absolute clarity. Nothing has ever felt so real as that experience did.'

Dennis turned to the class.

'Well, class, given what we have just experienced from this end,' he indicated me, 'our subject is either an Oscar-winning actor, which I don't for a minute think he is, or we have just witnessed something quite profound.

He has given us so much information that it should be relatively easy to trace. That period of history has been quite well documented.

Dennis turned and asked me, 'have you ever studied the era you have been talking about?'

'No,' I replied. 'I was a student pilot in my twenties, flying 48 hours before quitting. I also watched a television series called *Wings*, which was about British World War 1 pilots. That must have been sometime in the eighties. That is it. Other than that, I knew about the Red Baron via that song *Snoopy's Christmas*.'

'You have never read books about the Red Baron or World War 1 pilots?'

'I didn't even know there were such books,' I replied.

Dennis turned to the class.

'Any questions from the class?'

Every hand in the room shot up.

Luke asked, 'Were you aware of being in two places, like in the chair here in 1995 and also back there?'

'I was aware at the start and end and maybe, at one stage in the middle, of being here in the chair in 1995. The rest of the time, I was definitely back in that time. I don't think for a minute I will ever be able to fully describe the emotions and feelings that I have just experienced.'

'Dennis, I noticed his face changed, particularly around the mouth and jawline. His voice also changed. I know you commented on it earlier in the regression, but could you explain it again?' asked Joel.

Dennis sighed,' I have only seen it once before, but I have heard of it a bit more. When someone really locks into a significant past life experience, they sometimes manifest physical and emotional traits of the past life person. That is what we saw here.'

I tentatively put my own hand up,' Dennis, what I have just experienced felt very real to me, but the experience has shaken my core beliefs. You see, I don't, or should I say didn't, believe in past lives or reincarnation. What really happened here?'

Dennis said, 'Two-thirds of the world believe in reincarnation, particularly in the East. Most people in the Middle East or the West do not believe in reincarnation. So those in the East would say that you lived that life.'

He paused to gather his thoughts, then continued.

'In the West, some people would explain it away by saying that you created an imaginary scene as a method of therapy for things that have happened in your own life and that the emotions you displayed were parallel emotions that you have experienced in this life. However, I discount that theory, as I have witnessed too many regressions with too much detail.

'Your regression, if we research the time frame, I am sure, will provide far too much detail to be anything other than correct. So that leaves a belief in reincarnation or the contacting of the spirit of the said pilot, which would mean you had channelled him.'

I felt baffled, 'What is channelling?'

'It is where a spirit enters your body and speaks through you while you are in a trance. A more widely known practice is where people are able to either see or hear spirits and channel messages from them while still in a state of normality. People with this ability are known as psychics.'

'So, what do you think actually happened?' I asked.

Dennis smiled. 'Personally, I think I have come to believe in reincarnation. I have seen so many regressions with so much detail, and so many phobias and problems cured through the regressions, that I don't believe for a minute that so many spirits could be channelled and so many problems cured.'

I looked around the class. Everyone was very thoughtful. There was no doubt that the evening had been very thought-provoking and, in most cases, had completely upended many of our prior held beliefs.

Joel asked me, 'Do you think you will try and research this and find out if this Kurt and the other pilots you named actually existed?'

'I think I really do need to do this, even if it is for my own sanity, but I don't know where to start.'

Dennis interrupted, 'Go to the history department in the library and look up the Red Baron and anything to do with the World War 1 German pilots. I am sure you will find historical non–fiction books there.'

He continued, 'Now, class, we are already well past our normal finish time, so we will call it quits for the night and see you all next week, where we will delve into how to handle regressions for affecting cures of phobias.' He turned to me and thanked me for volunteering, adding, 'I did not for a minute think we would have an experience of this magnitude.'

The class all stood and applauded me. I could feel myself blushing and saying good night to my classmates, I got out of there pretty smartly.

At home, I sat down and told my wife the story.

'It is unbelievable,' she said, then asked, 'Do you really think I was your Maria?'

I looked into her eyes and realised with a great deal of awe, that I was looking into the same eyes that I recalled so vividly. Further, I was looking at the same face. 'Without a doubt,' I replied.

'We have to research it. What an incredible story.'

CHAPTER 13

## The Research

THE RESEARCH turned out to be easier than we thought. We found a book about Pour le Mérite winners in World War I and found the name Kurt Wolff listed as the 18th Pour le Mérite recipient with a total of 33 victories.

We also found Lothar and Manfred von Ricthofen listed along with Werner Voss, Karl Schafer and Carl Allmenroder. A second book that we found gave the history of the early days of Jasta 11 and the history of the first fighter wing made up of Jastas 10, 11, 4 and 6.

The original pilots of Jasta 11 were Kurt Wolff, Carl and Wilhelm Allmenroder, Sebastion Festner, Konstantin Kreft, Eduard Lubbert, Georg Simon. Manfred von Ricthofen, Karl (Charlie) Schafer and Lothar von Ricthofen arrived shortly after.

The only two to survive past the 1920s was Willi Allmenroder, who later married his brother Carl's fiancée and Georg Simon, who had become a prisoner of war.

The first commanding officer was Rudolf Lang, the

second Manfred von Ricthofen. Later pilots included an Otto Brauneck, Willi Rheinhard, and Hans Wolff (no relation).

A Werner Voss was appointed commander of Jasta 10 at a later date.

All the first names of these people had been mentioned in the regression. All were friends of Kurt Wolff. Manfred did have a wolfhound, and its name was Moritz!

The details supplied in the regression were correct on the whole, even in the number of his close friends, victories and medals.

Kurt Wolff was brought up by his uncle and aunty, and he did have a fiancée by the name of Maria Martha Bomeleit.

As a trainee clinical hypnotherapist and the guinea pig in the regression, I was absolutely stunned by what I, along with my wife, had found out.

How could I have known all this stuff? Was it lodged in my subconscious mind, or had I indeed channelled someone?

Further research found that the colours the planes had been painted by the first pilots were also pretty accurate. Again, I was blown away. In a book we found, the last flight of Kurt Wolff was described fairly accurately by one of his attackers and tallied with what I had described, but no mention was made of a weak top wing.

Exactly a week later, on September 23rd, around the same time of day, Werner Voss was killed in a similar action in the other prototype triplane fighting several British planes by himself in what has become a legendary aerial battle of World war 1.

Both planes were stressed to the maximum by aerial aerobatics during their final fights. A month or two later, another crash and a couple of forced landings identified a weakness in the top wing of the Fokker triplane due to poor workmanship. These resulted in further deaths and serious injury.

Lothar von Ricthofen was one of the injured and was incapacitated for a long time. Was the weak top wing a factor in the battle crashes of Kurt and Werner? We will never know.

In another book, we found a description of Kurt Wolff's physical appearance which dovetailed with mine at the same age, and my own character and personality also dovetailed with Kurt Wolff's own character and personality as described in various books that we found.

The final nail in the coffin for us was when we lined up a photograph of Kurt Wolff against one of myself at the same age. Although my photo sported fashionably long hair, there was no doubting the similarity in looks, particularly around the eyes.

My wife and I were staggered with what we had found out.

Had I really been Kurt Wolff in an earlier life, or had I channelled a spirit in the strongest possible way, as possibly suggested.

How did my wife and Maria fit together? I did a trace on my current ancestors and found that I had German blood on both my dad's and my mum's sides of my family through my great grandparents.

Had I connected with a lost distant relative? Looking at photos of the pilots, we were amazed to find one of my cousins looked incredibly like Charlie Schafer, and one of my nephews bears a strong likeness to Werner Voss!

To this day, I do not know the answers, but whatever the truth is, this is a story of a gentle young man who lived, loved and died as one of Germany's early young fighter pilots.

To have experienced the regression was one of the most amazing and emotional experiences of my life. To this day, I feel honoured to have experienced what I did.

This is a story that I became so involved with that it has haunted me for the last 27 years.

One morning, exactly one year after the regression, I woke up and took pen to paper and wrote a very long poem about the regression I had experienced. From where it came, I do not know. It just flowed out of me.

### Across the Bleeding Sky
*(written September 15th, 1996)*

> *The mysteries of the mind hold the key to the
> past.
> Beginning to unwind, my worries leave at
> last,
> Moving through the night, back through
> time and space,
> Could this be right? I've arrived, where is this
> place?*

> *Lord, look at me I'm flying,*

*Lord, look at me, time is flying,*
*Lord, look at me; where am I flying to?*

*Standing on a field, standing here at last,*
*What will this yield as I gaze upon my past?*
*Through the mist, I see the planes standing in*
    *a row,*
*My mind recalls the names somehow, I seem*
    *to know*

*Lord, look at me; why aren't I flying?*
*Lord, look at me. I wish I was flying,*
*Lord, look at me. I should be flying.*

*I'm walking across the grass with my mind*
    *racing back,*
*Above planes roar past, I hear the enemy*
    *flak,*
*I grasp my leader's hand, Manfred is his*
    *name.*
*He leads his gallant band, I'm at war; this is*
    *no game.*

*Lord, look at me; I'm flying,*
*Lord, look at me. I'm really flying,*
*Lord, look at me. I'm really flying high.*

*I'm flying through the air with the Baron at*
    *my side,*
*Feeling no fear and I'm bursting with*
    *pride,*

*We're flying to their lair, the enemy cannot*
    *hide,*
*Tommies beware, we've got God on our side.*

*Lord, look at me I'm flying,*
*Lord, look at me I'm firing,*
*Lord, look at me I'm firing at them.*

*The planes are twisting against the*
    *raging sky,*
*The heat it is blistering as I watch a*
    *Tommie die,*
*My guns, are crashing, Lord they must be*
    *hurting,*
*As my bullets are smashing, is this their final*
    *curtain?*

*Lord, look at me I'm flying,*
*Lord, look at me I see them dying,*
*Lord, look at them; they're dying.*

*Our planes we've painted red as our score*
    *begins to mount,*
*The Tommies live in dread as we increase*
    *our deadly count,*
*We're eagles in the sky, heroes of our land,.*
*We're living on a high, the Baron's invincible*
    *band.*

*Lord, look at us we're flying,*
*Lord look at us we're really flying,*

*Lord, look at us we're flying high.*

*My tally starts to grow as they fall before*
*    my gun,*
*The honours start to flow for the hero I've*
*    become,*
*I lead a charmed life as my friends start to*
*    crash,*
*Death is becoming rife like a rapidly*
*    spreading rash.*

*Lord, look at me I'm still flying,*
*Lord, look at me my friends are dying,*
*Lord, look at me I'm crying.*

*The day is a waning as I fly the skies alone,*
*The guns send a warning, one I should have*
*    known,*
*I turn to face my foe, three planes or is it*
*    four?*
*The enemy seems to have grown, Oh, Lord,*
*    here comes some more.*

*Lord, look at me I'm flying,*
*Lord, today I may face dying,*
*Lord, look at me I'm really trying.*

*My guns they are smashing as I spin my*
*    plane around,*
*One Tommie is a crashing as I fire another*
*    round,*

*The sky is full of planes as I roll around*
*    again,*
*Then I see the flames, and I feel a stabbing*
*    pain.*

*Lord, look at me I'm flying,*
*Lord, look at me, am I dying?*
*Lord, look at me I'm still trying.*

*I spin towards the ground with the enemy on*
*    my tail,*
*I flick my plane around, tracer flies by like*
*    hail,*
*I turn back to fight, my guns fire again,*
*I'm in a serious plight as I feel the hurting*
*    pain.*

*Lord, look at me I'm still flying,*
*Lord, look at me I'm dying,*
*Lord, look at me I really am crying.*

*My plane is smoking as I try to gain some*
*    height,*
*The engine is broken, as I try for level flight,*
*The cowling is burning as my plane begins to*
*    fall,*
*Sadness turns to yearning as I see my funeral*
*    pall.*

*Lord, look at me I'm still trying,*
*Lord, look at me I'm dying,*

*Lord, look at me I really am dying.*

*The pain comes creeping and rolls like a*
*wave,*
*God, I'm a weeping for the life that I crave,*
*Now I'm really paying for the world's*
*greatest sin,*
*Lord, for mankind I'm praying as my life*
*fades from within.*

*Lord, look on the ground I'm lying,*
*Lord, look why aren't I flying?*
*Lord, look they tell me I'm dying.*

*A voice is calling me, it's calling me at last,*
*If only I could see it's from the future, not the*
*past,*
*The words are from on high, through aeons of*
*time they roam,*
*Telling me not to die, 'cause it's time to come*
*on home.*

*Lord, look at me my soul is flying,*
*Lord, look at me I'm not crying,*
*Lord, look at me am I dying?*

*Moving through the night forward through*
*time and space,*
*Closer to the light, left behind that other*
*place,*

*In the present I now find the answers start to*
*flow,*
*I realise my mind has more lives than I will*
*know.*

*Lord, look at me I was dying,*
*Lord, look there's no need for crying,*
*Lord, look life is awe-inspiring.*

# *Afterword*

I FIRST CAME ACROSS this story in 1995.

This is the story of two truths.

Yes, the regression did take place along with three subsequent regressions. I was the recipient of all of them, and a huge amount of detail was given, leaving no doubt in one's mind that the pilot in question was Kurt Wolff when compared to the research uncovered.

The research showed that Kurt Wolff lived and died very much as I described, when under hypnotic past life regressions. In this narrative, I have written the story in the first person and tried to capture the feelings and emotions and story as I experienced them.

The time and date of 5.05pm, September 15th, has assumed some significance. I did actually learn to fly through 1975 and 1976, and my last flight ended at 5.05pm, September 15th 1976.

Kurt Wolff was shot down and killed at 5.05pm, September 15th 1917. The regression took place at 7.00pm, September 15th 1995.

Coincidence? Or something else?

The names of the modern-day characters in this narrative have been changed for privacy reasons, but without them, this book would not have happened.

As it is, from regression to publishing date, it has taken me some twenty–seven years to publish this story. I first put pen to paper and wrote this narrative in 2012.

From there, it has sat in my drawer until now. It is a story that both haunts me and fascinates me to this day. It poses more questions than it solves, and I still don't know the answers, but we leave it to the reader to decide what they believe.

I hope you have enjoyed the story and the courage of the young flier, Kurt Wolff. If nothing else, his story deserved to be told. It reflects the lives of many of the young aviators of World War 1, their battles, their friendships, their loves and their deaths.

So many of them had similar stories, and so many of them perished.

It was such a waste of young lives.

*D.R. Jessen 2022.*

# The Pilots and Their Victories

**Legend:**

*KIA: Killed in action. KIAC: Killed in aircraft crash*

## Rittmeister (Captain) Manfred von Ricthofen

KIA 21/4/18, aged 25

Kills: 80

**Awards**

Prussian Pour le Mérite, Prussian Order of the Red Eagle, Prussian Royal House Order of Hohenzollern Knights Cross, Prussian Iron Cross 1st class. Prussian Iron Cross 2nd class, Barvarian Military Merit Order, Duke Carl Eduard Medal with swords, War Merit Cross, Brunswick War Medal Cross, Saxon Military Order of St Henry Knight's Cross, Wurttemburg Military Merit Order Knight's Cross, Saxe–Ernestine House of Order Knight 1st Class with Swords, Hesse General Honour Decoration, Lippe War Honour Cross, Bremen Hanseatic Cross, Lubeck Hanseatic Cross, Hamburg Hanseatic Cross, Austrian Order of the Iron Crown, Austrian Military Merit

Cross, Bugarian Order of Bravery, Turkish Imtiaz Medal, Turkish Liakat Medal.

### Leutnant Werner Voss

KIA 23/9/17, aged 20

Kills: 48

**Awards**

Prussian Pour le Mérite, Prussian Royal House Order of Hohenzollern Knight's Cross, Prussian Iron Cross 1st Class, Prussian Iron Cross 2nd Class.

### OberLeutnant Lothar von Richthofen

KIAC 4/7/22, aged 27

Kills: 40

**Awards**

Prussian Pour le Mérite, Royal House Order of Hohenzollern Knight's Cross, Prussian Iron Cross 1st Class, Prussian Iron Cross 2nd Class, Barvarian Military Merit Order, Hamburg Hanseatic Cross, Turkish Liakat Medal.

### OberLeutnant Kurt Wolff

KIA 15/9/17, aged 22

Kills: 33

**Awards**

Prussian Pour le Mérite, Prussian Royal House Order of Hohenzollern Knight's Cross, Prussian Iron Cross 1st Class, Prussian Iron Cross 2nd Class, Barvarian Military Merit Medal with Swords.

### Leutnant Karl Allemroder

KIA 27/6/17, aged 21

Kills: 30

**Awards**

Prussian Pour le Mérite, Prussian Royal House Order of Hohenzollern Knight's Cross, Prussian Iron Cross 1st Class, Prussian Iron Cross 2nd Class, Grand Duchy of Oldenburgs Friedrich–August Cross, Bayerische Militar Kronen Orden.

### Leutnant Karl (Charlie) Schafer

KIA 5/6/17, aged 25

Kills: 30

**Awards**

Prussian Pour le Mérite, Prussian Royal House Order of Hohenzollern Knight's Cross, Prussian Iron Cross 1st Class, Prussian Iron Cross 2nd Class, Barvarian Military Merit Medal with Swords.

### Hauptmann (Captain) Willi Reinhard

KIAC 6/7/18, aged 27

Kills: 20

**Awards**

Prussian Royal House of Hohenzollern Knight's Cross, Prussian Iron Cross 1st Class, Prussian Iron Cross 2nd Class.

### Leutnant Otto Brauneck

KIA 26/7/17, aged 21

Kills:10

**Awards**

Prussian Royal House Order of Hohenzollern Knight's Cross, Prussian Iron Cross 1st Class, Prussian Iron Cross

2nd Class.

## Sergeant Sebastion Festner
KIA 25/4/17, aged 22

Kills: 12

### Awards
Cross of a Member with Swords. (Top NCO award), Prussian Iron Cross 1st Class, Prussian Iron Cross 2nd Class.

## Leutnant Konstantin Krefft
Survived the war

Kills: 4

## Leutnant Willi Allemroder
Survived the war

Kills: 2

## Main combat aircraft flown by Kurt Wolff:
Fokker triplane, Albatross and Halberstadt

## Enemy aircraft types shot down by Kurt Wolff:
FE2b–1, Sopwith Camel, FE8, Morane, Spad, BE.2c, Nieuport 11, Se5a, Sopwith triplane, RE8, Martinside, Bristol, DH4 bomber.

Printed in Great Britain
by Amazon